CASSIEL

CASSIEL

ROGUE ANGELS
BOOK TWO

LILITH DARVILLE

eBook ISBN: 978-1-998127-23-8
Paperback ISBN: 978-1-998127-24-5

Cover Design by Atra Luna Design (www.atraluna.de)
Editing by Maggie Morris, The Indie Editor (www.indieeditor.ca)
Formatting by Kate Tilton's Author Services, LLC (www.katetilton.com)

BLACK ROSE AND THE THREE PRINCES

Believing Black Rose lost a decade ago, Lord Syrael asked the mirror once again: "Magic mirror on the wall, who is the most powerful sex angel lord of all?" As Black Rose had come of age, Syrael started to lose his power. The mirror told Syrael that Black Rose could kill him, but if he gained her power, Syrael would be the most powerful demon in the land. The mirror also showed her hiding in the forest with the three sex angel princes.

The archangel was furious that he'd been tricked and decided to retrieve Black Rose himself, planning to steal her power and kill her. First, he appeared at the cabin disguised as a peddler and offered Black Rose a silky black bustier as a present. He laced the bustier so tightly, Black Rose collapsed from lack of oxygen. The princes returned just in time to loosen the laces and revive her. Next, the demon lord dressed as a perfume salesman with a fragrance specifically designed for her and convinced Black Rose to try a squirt laced with a powerful poison. Once again, the princes discovered Black Rose before the poison took full effect and revived her by washing the scent from her body.

Finally, the archangel disguised himself as a farmer and offered Black Rose a drugged apple. Black Rose hesitated before accepting it, so Syrael cut the apple in half, keeping the harmless half for himself. After watching Syrael eat without consequence, Black Rose took a large bite and immediately fell into a state of suspended animation, causing the archangel to think he had triumphed. This time, the princes were unable to find an antidote to the magical elixir.

CASSIEL

Fuck! Fuck! Fuck! Aleah's rapid heart rate warns me she has her head in a toilet long before I reach her. The power to read the heartbeats of others comes in handy at times. If I didn't love my brothers, I'd kill them for putting our team in this position.

We're the three royal princes of Nirvana, called to serve the gods as sex angel lords. It's not a job, it's a vocation, although you'd never know it the way my brothers are behaving. Both are more than capable of shielding themselves from the negative effects of physical illness. My gut tells me Troy's not as affected by Aleah's sickness as he pretends to be unless you count being love sick. Whatever the two of them hope will happen by leaving me alone with Aleah simply won't happen. I know a problem when I see one.

I detour through the kitchen where Tristan put Aleah's medications. *Fuck.* Whose bright idea was it to put me in a caregiver role? Which pills should I give her? I take a chance and grab the anti-nausea tablets, pain meds, and a glass of water. By the time I reach the bedroom, Aleah's curled into a ball on the bed, eyes squeezed tight, and her small form takes me back to when she was a young girl in the forest. The corresponding tug on my heartstrings proves I'm not the cold-hearted bastard my brothers accuse me of being or that I portray.

"I brought your pills." I read off the names on the bottles for good measure.

I barely catch her muffled response. "One of each, please."

I shake a pill from each bottle into my palm then place them in the small brown hand that lies open on the bed. She dry swallows the pills refusing the water I offer. A strangled sound follows that I take to be thanks. I close the built-in blinds and light a candle to read by. Again, I curse the gods for being less than forthcoming about the angelic mating bond.

I settle on the bed beside Aleah without touching her, open the Double Diary to the bookmarked page and start reading aloud. I'm expecting the magic woven into the words to affect Aleah. What I'm not anticipating is their impact on me. The more I read in their diary, the more insight I have about what drew Atroyel to Aleah. The sexual and emotional passion they have for each other survived life's many hurdles and grew to a blazing fire. Their unconditional love for each other is evident even to a realist like me. Their outpouring of feeling flows over me like fine wine opening my palate to take in hidden undertones. It appears that Aleah took years to break through Atroyel's moody exterior, yet I have no sense of her berating or criticizing him. She seems to accept him for what he is.

Aleah seems to have shown Atroyel a way to express his feelings, and instead of weakening him, she's given him a way to face the world. As I read on, I can't remain blind to the gift Aleah's given Troy. Her love is pure and without artifice. The magic Atroyel wove into the words would reveal any hidden agendas. Her entries clearly show a depth of love for my brother that pierces my cynical core.

> "Life with you hasn't always been easy, but it's always been real."
> "I don't want you to feel regret. Not ever!"
> "I'll fight for you until I'm forced to let go!"
> "I fought to get you back."

As I read on, I'm left with so many questions: her feelings about motherhood, what had threatened their relationship, how had she fought to get Troy back? Their diary reveals a level of emotional exposure I rarely see between couples. They'd both risked fallout from leaving themselves so vulnerable to one another.

Slowly, Aleah's body uncurls as the words from the diary fall from my lips. While I read the words, she snuggles against me and rests her hand on my bare forearm. Electricity sizzles through me the instant her skin touches mine. My heart skips for a split second before I remember her rejection and remind myself of how she's disrupting our work. That puts things back in perspective, and I put the shock down to the quick movement of electrons in the air, nothing more.

Despite my best intentions to stay clear of her, my curiosity about this woman grows the more I read. I'm usually one for the big picture, but suddenly I want the details about what makes Aleah tick. I stop reading aloud for a moment and focus in on the entry dated September 1. Troy finds her to be distant, and who the fuck is Nick that he refers to? I push back the finger of jealousy that flickers as I read his name.

"I'm a mess, yet I'm strong and capable." I can't help but smile at her insight about herself. That hits the proverbial nail on the head when describing this fascinating woman. I quickly turn the pages searching for her hidden agenda. I'd learned through a millennium as a sex angel that most people have one, and I've seen the good, the bad, and the ugly. I have no doubt that if I look long and hard enough, I'll find hers, and the push-pull between her and Troy fascinates me.

When she writes about experiencing palpitations and tingles, my mind goes on high alert. This is the first indication of her powers breaking through the binding spell suppressing her magic. I read on, fighting harder and harder to convince myself my curiosity is strictly strategical. She's taped a sticky note from Troy over the end of one of his fantasies. For a reason I can't even begin to fathom, it's his sticky note that makes my heart ache.

Hi My Love!
My heart aches too, but that's not true. My ache is a little lower. You can pleasure yourself as long as you think of me. Gotta run errands—see you later. Thinking of you! Love Me.
:-)

I flip ahead several pages and notice sticky notes sprinkled throughout. As if sharing their love through the diary isn't enough, they have to leave each other sappy notes as well. Yet something in my cold heart yearns to have someone to exchange sappy notes with.

Morning Love:
Think of me as I do you! Again—smile—it's Friday. Soon Saturday. . .
Are you going to let me
PLAY?

To which she responds:

Am I ever! I've been waiting for this all week. Last night, I had a prelude. . .

"I guess I'm not any good at come-hither looks." I glom onto this first sign of artifice. She presents if as a flaw, but I know better.

I close my eyes as the power of what these two share hits me. Something makes Aleah stir, and she snuggles closer against me tightening her grasp on my forearm. She sighs as if taking comfort from my heat. Blue grace rises from her skin coating mine, and I could swear there's a slight sensation of heat in my left shoulder. Slapping the fanciful thought away, I get back to business. The sooner I figure out how we're going to deal with the complications the mating bond brings to our lives, the better for all of us. And one thing I know for sure, Aleah will never be part of our team. I won't allow it. I'm incredibly talented at spotting any skills and strengths beneficial to helping us attain our mission, and this woman doesn't have them. Instead, she's a distraction. I'd been willing to overlook her intrusion for Troy's sake, but now she's snatched Tristan and brings nothing but chaos.

Ali moans and moves restlessly beside me as if sensing my thoughts. The interruption brings me back to the job at hand, reading this damned diary. As I work my way through another of Atroyel's convoluted passages, it doesn't surprise me that he came up with the idea of writing a joint diary; after all, word bestowal is his most potent power.

What's startling is the depth of sexuality, passion, and commitment these two have been willing to explore, how deeply they've exposed their soft underbellies. I doubt that I'd be willing to leave myself this vulnerable with anyone, yet I envy their deep and enduring bond. And now, the universe has given Tristan a matching gift, allowed him to share in their love. I shake off all this emotional foolishness and get back to the diary. The only love in the cards for me is the love I help create as a sex angel lord.

I need to focus on what I'm here to do and find out Aleah's weaknesses and triggers to teach her how to protect herself against Syrael. I'm not doing this for her; I'm doing it for my brother. Once we get rid of Syrael, I can get the hell away from this Nephilim and the irrational thoughts she provokes.

I run through what I've learned so far, and I have a lot of work to do. I think showing her how to protect herself against Syrael's manipulations will prove to be a more significant challenge than I imagined. Her self-esteem is far lower than her demeanor would suggest, and she has a large rejection complex and multiple hang-ups. However, these are the cards I'm dealt, so I'll play my best hand. I have to at least look like I'm trying with her. I won't give Atroyel any ammunition to put in that acerbic tongue. So far, the only area I have to work with is role play. Whenever I read about their fantasies and role-plays, more grace rises from Aleah. One thing is patently clear, my brother's fear of hurting his beloved has kept him from seeing what Aleah needs. *Fuck off, Cassiel.* I berate myself for all of this foolish talk. What goes on between those two is none of my business.

Aleah's next line, "I need your love! It makes me whole," does nothing to soften my hardened heart. I shouldn't begrudge my brothers a love like this . . . But I do.

But it's Atroyel's declaration that brings me to my knees.

> ### My Love
> *She was a lover whose mind never strayed far from*
> *the scene.*
> *All the power pieces concealed in me responded*
> *fivefold.*

Our open boldness of speaking out and then usually
*   acting it out was astonishing.*
It got so that the mere touching of one another while
*   walking past each other could set off a confla-*
*   gration.*
As apprehension faded to trust, a cool sweetness
*   settled over us.*
Time, thank God, stood still.

I slam the book shut, unable to go on.

2

———

ALEAH

One minute, I'm having the best wet dream of my life and the next, I'm awake, instantly aware I'm snuggled up against someone who isn't Troy or Tristan. Cass. *Shit!* As consciousness floods back, I bolt upright and scooch over on the bed while I meet Cass's golden gaze.

"Sorry." I throw the word out to cover any embarrassment I've caused Cass by vomiting or something equally mortifying in front of this man who so obviously dislikes me.

"For?" Cass raises an eyebrow in the same way his brothers do.

I look around for my glasses. Anything to avoid Cass's penetrating stare. "I'm sorry if I did anything to make you uncomfortable. Sometimes the onset of a migraine is pretty extreme." That's as good a euphemism as any to cover the purge that precedes most of my migraines.

"No problem." Cass holds out my glasses, giving me a looking-for-these questioning gaze. At least he's semi-civil for a change. Grateful, I take my shield and slide it into place. I definitely need it to deal with the negative vibes rolling from him. I give him a small smile of thanks because that's the polite thing to do. Sprint away like a startled fawn would only add fuel to the fire of this already rocky relationship. I don't know what it is about Troy and his family members, these and the human ones, but, besides Tristan, they tolerate me because they have to. But I'm not family, not really. Troy and I had talked about my hunger to be part of a family. Our discussions typically ended the same way.

"Beauty, if you ever needed help, they'd be there for you."

He just didn't understand that being family meant more than being helpful. It involved a connection and love I've only had with Troy.

And now, Tristan. My soul-mate connection lets me know my guys aren't near, but they're still close enough for me to detect. Both emit calm contentment, and I have no doubt Troy is in one of his all-time favorite positions—stretched out on an outdoor lounger taking in the scenery. My radar tells me Tristan is with him, no doubt in a similar supine position. Not that I have a fucking clue whether Tristan is a sun worshiper like Troy. My heart does a wee cha-cha as I think about how much I have to learn about this new love of mine. I put that happy thought in my treasure chest to examine later.

Right now, I have Cass to deal with. I have to extricate myself from him without deepening the rift yawning between us. Troy made it clear with his human family that if they forced him to choose, I'd be his first and only choice. I've no doubt that if the subject came up, he'd do the same with Cass. Resolute, I lean into the discomfort of meeting the penetrating gaze that hasn't wavered. My intuition tells me something has changed while I slept, but I can't put my finger on what.

"Thank you so much for staying with me. I appreciate it. I hope I wasn't too much trouble." *Lame, Aleah.*

I could swear I see amusement flicker in those weird

golden eyes of his. "That depends on your definition of trouble."

I narrow my eyes as I try to read him, but I have no sense of whether he's joking or serious. I'm used to Troy saying things like this to get a reaction from me because he thinks I'm so cute when I'm all riled up. But that was his rather unique sense of humor. Cass seems to be missing the humor gene.

"Let's define it as anything that makes you uncomfortable; after all, you've been very clear what you think about the chaos I've brought down on you." The words are out of my mouth before I can snatch them back. I open my mouth to apologize for being bitchy.

"No need to apologize. I prefer people say what they mean, and what you say is true." Cass's mouth quirks into a rare smile. In one smooth move, he's off the bed and stretching that long, gorgeous body. "It's me who should apologize. What I said was uncalled for." Another twitch at the corners of his mouth. "You don't bring any more chaos than Atroyel and Tristan have at times." Cass pours a couple of glasses of something from a pitcher on the table and hands me a glass.

I take a sip of the same delicious coconut water concoction I'd had last night. The need to replenish fluids overcomes me, and I down the drink before handing it back to Cass. "Thanks, I needed that." I let those words hang in the air, assuming he'll think the thanks are for the drink when in fact, I'm acknowledging his extending a twig from his olive branch.

As Cass moves to the windows, I catch my reflection in the glass, my disheveled appearance coming into sharp focus. I hop off the bed and head toward the massive bathroom. "I'll just freshen up and meet you on the deck."

On the way to the double sinks facing the outdoor tub

and shower, I shed my shorts, top, and undies and slip into a beautiful teal silk kimono robe hanging on a large rack in the corner. I wash my face and lean toward the large mirror, surprised by the woman staring back at me. This confident woman looks ready to take on the world when I have no idea what I'm getting myself into with these guys.

Messy brown-black curls sticking up at random frame a face with the genetic gift of looking a lot younger than my forty years. Hell, I'd been asked to produce ID to verify I was of drinking age until a couple of years ago. I swipe a comb through my hair and give a nod to the woman in the mirror. *You'll do.* Despite the migraine hangover, my large brown eyes sparkle with anticipation.

As I spread lotion over my very smooth tawny skin, I thank the gods they gave me a perfectly symmetrical face. I might not be runway model beautiful, but there isn't much anyone can criticize about my face, unlike my body. I push aside my long list of deficits and run a comb through my hair, bringing it back to some semblance of order and give my face one last look. I'll do.

I head into my dressing room expecting to be alone, so my heart leaps to my throat, and I give a girlie shriek as I catch sight of a large male body in my peripheral vision. With a hand on my chest, I turn to face the intruder. Cass stands at the other entrance holding a very fitted black silk sheath with beautiful gold filigree at the neckline and sides. A pair of gold sandals and what looks like a black thong dangle from the other hand. "Wear these." That's it, just those two words. I open my mouth to argue and decide against it. Best not to risk breaking our fragile truce. I grab the items and give him my best you-can-leave-anytime look. He turns around but stays put.

"I'll be with you in just a moment." I try subtlety to no avail.

"What's the deal with this phone call that never happened you and Atroyel talk about in your diary?" Cass asks in that deep baritone that seems to make its way straight from the bottom of this throat to nestle in my G-spot. I give myself a mental eye roll. What the fuck am I doing? I don't even like this guy, but all of a sudden, all I can think about is how hot he is. What on earth is wrong with me? I have no idea how I'm going to keep two guys happy, never mind three.

"Where did that come from? Why would you pick that to talk about?" Deflection's always been one of my best weapons.

"Atroyel brings it up in the diary more than once, so I figure there's a potential weakness Syrael can exploit," Cass replies easily.

Ensuring his back remains turned, I shimmy into the thong before removing the silky robe. I slip into the dress but before I can fight with the zipper, Cass steps behind me and inches the zipper up my back. Another of those weird sparks of electricity shoots through me as his finger touches my bare skin. I suck in a quiet breath and try to focus on Cass's question.

There's only one section of our diaries that discuss a phone call, and I clearly remember the situation. "Troy went to visit his friend for a weekend after a particularly intensely emotional week between us. We'd revealed inner secrets that had left us feeling vulnerable, and I'd yearned for him and thought he'd be doing the same. I prayed for him to call, but he never did." I step away from Cass when he finishes with the zipper and thank the gods as a tropical breeze cuts through the heat between us.

"So, why didn't you call him? You don't strike me as the type of woman who sits around wringing her hands and waiting for something to happen," Cass says. "I'm sure Troy would have been happy to talk to you."

I give him a wry smile as I remember Troy's reaction to my emotional meltdown about the missed phone call. "That's what he said at the time too, but it had been a long-standing, unspoken rule between us that I didn't try to contact him when he was on one of his getaways unless I needed something." I slip the gold Grecian sandals on my feet to avoid his gaze.

"It certainly sounds as if you needed something from the exchange in your diary." Cass heads toward the door and pauses at the entrance. "Coming?"

"That's what Troy said," I mutter as I follow. "He went on about it at length in the diary, but you know that. You two are more alike than you think."

3

CASSIEL

I find Troy and Tristan arranging various dishes on one of the suite's dining tables with a terrific view of the grounds below and ocean beyond. Both brothers turn and gape when Aleah walks in behind me. Tristan gives a wolf whistle and strides over to her with arms spread . . . then stops dead, mere inches in front of her. "May I, mistress?" He steps back and gives a sweeping bow.

"You may, sire." Aleah giggles and gives a small curtsy. Tristan gathers her in his arms and gives her a bear hug and deep kiss, then leads her to the table. "Does this mean I'm forgiven?" He waits for her to slide onto the banquette beside Troy, then takes his place beside her. The two of them cocoon her as if they need to protect her from the big bad wolf—me.

"Feeling better, beauty?" Troy grips the back of her neck and touches his forehead to hers.

"Much." Aleah looks at me and smiles. "Whatever Cass did must have worked. My headache's gone, and I'm starving."

I take an end seat and cross my hands on the table to stop

from drumming them while the two of them fuss over Aleah with offers of food and drink. Although I respond to their small talk, I'm focused on my plan. I've come up with a way to get into Aleah's head, so I can uncover her hidden agenda while protecting myself from being influenced by her magic. Despite Tristan's romantic belief in destiny, history has shown that angelic mating bonds rarely exist. It's one thing to believe Troy's bond with her after what they've shared, but an instant connection strong enough to form a mating bond — like the one she's supposed to have with Tristan — is unheard of. It's beyond belief that she'd have a connection with both brothers that I don't share. All I need is some time alone with her and a way to remove her subconscious barriers so I can access her subconscious and memories.

When Troy and Tristan are finally satisfied that Aleah's well taken care of, they help themselves and pass the serving plates to me. Although I attempt to train my attention everywhere but on her, I'm hyper-aware of every movement Aleah makes.

"You're a stunner in that dress, *mon chou*," Tristan says.

I stop myself from snorting at the sap these two are pouring on Aleah. If I learned anything from the diary, Aleah needs a master to take her in hand, not all this gushy stuff.

I'm more than a little envious, although wild horses won't drag that confession out of me. I need to remember my prime directives to keep my brothers safe and carry out our mission as sex angel lords. It's not as if I'm looking for a romantic relationship. I've lived quite happily without one, except for a short but intense infatuation several centuries ago. Despite being sex angels and being an active part of the kink scene, we rarely meet women who stimulate more than our baser sexual needs. This is particularly true for me, although unlike my brothers, I maintain a very active sex life. I'm all for satisfying baser needs.

"Are you ready to finish the conversation we started earlier, beauty?" Troy brings the small talk to an abrupt close as usual.

"Is it true what you said earlier? About sex angel lords being able to spank someone without prior consent?" Aleah turns her attention to me and seems to have no problem shifting gears.

"Are you accusing me of lying?" I keep my expression neutral and ignore the sharp looks I get from both brothers.

Aleah frowns as my dart hits its mark. "That's not what I meant. It's just that it doesn't make sense to me. You said your mission is to use sex for good and virtue and all that, and the first rule of sexuality is consent. Risk-aware consensual kink, that's the tenet, right? I didn't give my consent for Tristan to spank me." She continues a dissertation on consent as if defending her doctoral thesis. Troy and Tristan hide their amusement behind food consumption.

"And before you start in on me about implied consent, let me remind you that only happens once we've set hard and soft limits. I've done my research. And would you take a man over your knee? No. Well, why not? I'm sure you've run into men needing punishment at some point in your long and illustrious career as sex angels." Oh yes, she's on a roll with her synapses firing on all cylinders.

"You're right. I wouldn't put them over my knee. I'd use a spanking bench. Would you prefer that?" I use my formidable Dom tone, the one that lets my subs know I mean business.

"I'd prefer to be asked before being manhandled." Aleah is oblivious to my commanding tone.

Troy waves his fork in the air. "That's a good segue to resume our talk about our limits. After all, that's one of the reasons we're here, to figure out what leaves Ali open to Lord Syrael's attack." Troy nods at Aleah. "You said spanking as punishment is a hard limit for you, but what about when it's part of a role play? As I recall, spanking and flogging make you dripping wet. You begged for more. What's changed?"

That snaps my attention to Aleah with laser focus. There'd been no mention of any kink activities in the entries we'd read so far, so this comes as a surprise, as does the crimson rimming the shell of her ears. This reaction sends my curiosity up a few notches.

Aleah clears her throat. "Nothing's changed. That was different." She grimaces so she knows how lame that sounds. Heaving one of her mighty sighs, she continues, "That's because I made it part of a role play in my head and it had nothing to do with the daddy-little-girl play." She straightens and points her finger at Troy as a thought occurs to her. "And you refused to pretend to punish me, remember? You'd flog me for stimulation, but not as part of a daddy scenarios."

This time it's Tristan who leans forward. "So, you wanted Troy to punish you, but he couldn't spank you? I'm confused."

"Get used to it," Troy says.

Aleah stabs his arm with her index finger and grins. "Bastard."

"Bitch goddess." He uses his index finger to push her shoulder.

"Ouch." Aleah stabs back. "That hurt." She's laughing, and the two of them go at it like kids in a schoolyard.

"Could you two focus?" Tristan cuts in before I have a chance. "This is serious. It will be easy for Lord Syrael to break through your defenses if you don't know your mind. Why is it all right for Troy to spank you but not me?" Tristan manages to sound wounded, although I very much doubt that he is. Since the mating bond activated, neither brother is behaving predictably. All I sense from him is intense curiosity . . . and a woody.

Aleah and Troy instantly shed all trace of humor.

"I do know my own mind." She gives the classic talk-to-the-hand gesture. "And before you go all high and mighty with me, I'll explain. Troy can spank or flog me during sex because I know he'd never hurt me. I trust him. And he knows my triggers and respects them. I might have liked punishment in a role play—"

"Your double diary makes it very clear you'd like punishment as part of a role-play." I'm not letting her off the hook.

"But role play isn't Troy's thing, so we never had to worry about it. I don't know you two, not really. I have no idea what punishment looks like for you, but I've had enough men lay hands on me to know it's might not be pleasant. I'm into sensation, not pain." She moves food around her plate to avoid the three sets of eyes trained on her. "You haven't earned the right."

4

ATROYEL

"You haven't earned the right." Aleah says this calmly, but inside she's teeming with conflicting emotions as she calculates how much to expose herself.

Cass glares back at her, but for once, he's caught off guard by her direct approach. Something's up with him, but I can't read him because an immunity shield spell blocks my way. I glance at Tristan, and he shrugs—the shield's blocking him as well. Cass leans forward, but Tristan cuts him off at the pass.

"You're right, babe, we haven't earned the right. That will take time, and we're on to something here. You said you need to visit BDSM clubs as part of the research for your articles, right?" Tristan holds a strawberry to her lips, and three pairs of eyes watch as she sucks in the fruit and licks the juice dribble on her bottom lip. "What would happen if, during a scene, your play partner pulled you over his or her knee? Knowing your response is exactly the kind of information we're looking for so we can help protect you from Lord Syrael."

Aleah responds without hesitation. "I'd use my safe word."

"Suppose your partner ignores your safe word?" I ask.

"I'd yell like hell for the dungeon monitor." Aleah gives a sharp nod to punctuate her statement.

"Not all clubs have dungeon monitors," Cass says. "You're restrained and at your master's mercy. What then?"

"All the research I've done states BDSM clubs have DMs, so that's not going to happen." Aleah makes a blanket statement, her favorite counter to an argument she doesn't have the answer for."

The extent of Aleah's BDSM experience includes attending two munches, one kink event, and a BDSM conference, so she's hardly the expert she's pretending to be. But my Aleah loves to play poker, and she can bluff with the best of them.

"I hate to disabuse you of that notion, but there are many clubs and events without dungeon monitors. That's one of the main reasons people must be aware of the risks before exploring the kink life. You aren't aware of the risks or your reactions, and that makes you vulnerable." Cass calls her bluff. "But just for the sake of argument, let's assume there isn't anyone to rescue you. What will you do then?"

"I'm not sure. I guess it would depend on the situation. Too bad there isn't a way to find out." Aleah brightens as she straightens. "Or is there? Using your magic? That would be a great way to start my series for work. I'd love to explore my reactions in a safe environment, but to do that, I'd have to suspend reality during the scene but remember everything that happens. That's not possible, is it?"

"I don't need magic to make you feel threatened," Cass says with absolute certainty, but he doesn't know Aleah.

"That won't work," Aleah replies with equal certainly.

"Why not? You have no idea what I'm capable of?" Cass uses the threatening tone I've seen give the gods pause.

"I have no doubt you use that lieutenant coronel attitude of yours to bring us mere mortals to our knees, but it won't work with me." Aleah doesn't flinch from Cass's aggressive gaze. "And the why not before you ask is simple. I know in my soul that you won't hurt me."

Waves of aggression roll from Cass as he leans forward, but Aleah doesn't back off despite the fear rolling through her.

"I know you have no love lost on me, but one thing you can't hide is your love for your brothers. You won't do anything to hurt one of them intentionally, and if you hurt me, you hurt them." Aleah stabs her pointer finger in Cass's direction. "I know that in here," she stabs her own chest. "Even though you detest me, you'll fight for me with your life because I'm part of what makes them whole. At least I am for Troy, so I assume it's the same for Tristan now that we're bonded." Despite the immunity shield protecting Cass's emotions, the arrow Aleah inadvertently releases pierces through, allowing a split-second of insight into his vulnerability. But he seals it shut before I have time to have a good look.

"And we won't know whether my reaction is tainted by my history and inhibitions unless we remove them. Isn't part of this exercise finding out who I truly am sexually?" Aleah punctuates her argument by stabbing the table in her classic take-that-sucker movement.

"Fine, have it your way." Cass crosses his arms over his chest as his emotional shutter clicks shut.

Not Aleah; her emotions are coming through loud and clear. She's almost bouncing with anticipation and excitement. She tips her head to the side like she does when giving a mental fist pump. "So, where do we start?"

Both Tristan and I snap to attention. Making her role-play character the only reality Aleah is aware of is well within our powers. "Great idea, beauty." I snap my fingers, not because I need to but to add to the drama of the moment, and paper appears in my hand. I place several sheets on the table with a pen. "Here's the standard BDSM checklist. Cass will take you through it while Tristan and I brainstorm a role play. How about we meet back here in a half-hour or so?"

As she nods consent, Aleah manages to look dismayed and intrigued. Cass looks like a predator about to play with his prey before devouring it. I tip Aleah's full lips to mine and murmur against them. "We won't be long. You love doing surveys. Have some fun."

Aleah's pout speaks volumes—we're leaving her to the shark—but she slides off the bench, and Tristan follows her. He pulls her into his arms for one of his signature hugs.

Once we're out of earshot, Tristan says, "He'll eat her alive."

I laugh, knowing my Aleah. "That may be, but by the time she's done with him, he'll feel as if she's stripped off several layers of skin. She has *command brain*—she'll tell the truth as she knows it and lives it, and she'll insist he does the same."

"With all her hard limits, it won't take long to go through the checklist," Tristan says.

"We've got time. Aleah will question almost every item and ask for definitions. Bets are that when all is said and done, she'll say she's willing to try small anal plugs, blindfolds, giving or receiving hand jobs, private nudity, being serviced sexually, light bondage, and cock worship. She'll make double penetration and gags a soft limit. The rest of the items on that lengthy checklist will be hard limits for her, especially anything that involves pain or force. As for role plays, she'll choose being auctioned to some rich guy for charity, kidnapping, and prison scenes," I say.

"All of those hard limits must have restricted your options when you were human," Tristan grumbles. Too many remove the freedom to play. "It will be a challenge to come up with a role play that will push her limits. She's damned near vanilla."

"That's where you're wrong. Aleah's list will change dramatically once she trusts. Then, she'll be willing to explore damn near anything that doesn't risk doing permanent damage," I say. "She once said she's afraid she's kinkier than I am. I ignored her fear at the time and didn't recognize it came from a place of shame rooted deeply in her mind. I'm not going to do that anymore. If she wants to explore, we'll help her navigate her way safely. Let's grab a drink and put together a scenario."

Tristan leads the way to the large wooden swing chair with yet another spectacular view of the Mediterranean Sea. We help ourselves to a couple of sweating bottles of beer sitting in a large ice bucket, and I pick up the pen and pad lying next to it.

"So, what do you have in mind for a role play?" I ask as I get ready to write. "Let's make it a good one. I have to admit I'm no longer afraid of Aleah's sexual appetites, and I'm looking forward to our new journey of discovery. How about something that gives Aleah some idea of what's in store for her at one of the kink events she says she has to attend. Any ideas?"

"Great idea. I think she has an event on Friday night so this can be a trial run. A win-win, as she's so fond of saying. She likes to write from first-hand experience, so I figure we come up with a role play that will expose her triggers and give her something to write about," I say.

"You know her better than I do? What does she like? What does she find triggering? Once we come up with a scenario, I can place the charm that will make the scene real. The spell will work best if I weave in details," Tristan says. "What do you have in mind?"

"It's always best to keep things simple with Aleah. She has such a huge wall of inhibitions, she'll do a good enough job of adding complications herself, and she'll question everything. I propose she be a reporter or businesswoman asking for her first kink experience." I conjure and don a pair of sunglasses.

"Which one of us will work the scene?" Tristan asks. "She's not going to respond well if we sic Cass on her."

"*Au contraire, mon frere,* I disagree. Cass is precisely the right person because she doesn't trust him on any level. And putting them together when they're most vulnerable is the best way to see just how he's involved in our mating bond.

5

CASSIEL

I open the folder on my lap and review the role play Atroyel and Tristan concocted for our first scene with Aleah. They'd looked very much like the cats that shared the canary as they'd presented the role play they'd cooked up. Something about Aleah seems to have given Tristan and Troy selective memory about who I am. I insist on free rein to shape the scene in whatever way I feel appropriate, and, in this circumstance, we've agreed the objective is to help protect Aleah. That's all the consent I need to do the mind probe that will take me beyond the fortress walls she's erected in her subconscious.

Since Aleah arrived, something interfered with my psychic connection with my brothers, but I can't put my finger on what that is. Before Atroyel left us to find Aleah, we could read each other's emotions and speak telepathically. Typically, the only reason we close ourselves off is mentally protect each other from harm, but ever since they've activated this godsdamn mating bond, I haven't had a clear read.

Much as I'd hated it, I'd had to wait for Troy and Tristan to reveal whatever hot plan they had in mind. Aleah had mumbled something about freshening up and fled as soon as Troy and Tristan were out of sight. I'd paced the deck while I considered and dismissed ways to get our team under control.

When Tristan and Troy were done concocting their scenario, we'd all met up on the upper deck, but I was oblivious to the magnificent view of the ocean. We sat on the low-slung couches, and Tristan opened a bottle of wine to toast Aleah's first experience with a Dom.

After what seemed like an excessive amount of time discussing consent and safe words, we'd all agreed on their role-play—a control-freak businesswoman looking for her first BDSM experience. Using our furniture creation powers, I've replicated one of the clubs on Aleah's list that caters to Doms and subs alike to start Aleah's training. As a Dom, I prefer master-slave sessions, but I've set up several viewing and playrooms to accommodate just about any fantasy or role-play. When we're ready to watch the scenes similar to what she'll see Friday night, I'll use the portal to take her to a real club.

I'm hugely into role play, and from what I learned reading the diary, so is Aleah. Or she could be if given a chance. I'm about to find out, and despite my better judgment, I'm looking forward to having Aleah all to myself without Atroyel and Tristan's overprotective presence.

I'm sitting in one of the viewing salons that is much like the viewing rooms seen in the movies, except the room it faces into is much larger. The salon itself has wide burnished walnut and alternating gold paneled walls, a cathedral ceiling crowned with a crystal chandelier, and gold- and black-veined marble floor. It's like stepping back into another era, the perfect setting for this role play.

I review the scenario we chose. Aleah's applied to be the play partner of a master Dom—me. Her profile tells me she's curious about everything and wants to discover the lifestyle. Tonight, she wants a chance to explore the world of bondage, discipline, domination, and submission firsthand.

My alter ego in this role play rarely finds a candidate who meets his *many* specifications. I snort, attributing the emphasis on the word to Atroyel. The scenario, written role play, tells me this one is precisely who I've been longing for. I'm to show her some scenes with the twofold objective of preparing her for what she'll see at the kink events and finding her hidden secrets. Yes, this role-play will do nicely, and I'll be whomever I damn well please.

Aleah's strut announces her arrival and shouts the mantra: *"I've got this."* The furtive glances as she takes of her surroundings tell a different story. The moment I see her, intuition sparks into flames of desire on a level I haven't felt in a very long time. That's saying something because I fuck a lot of women, whenever and however I can. That's one of the benefits of being a sex angel, showing woman how good it can be. But something about this woman burrows past my sexual needs and hammers on the locked door protecting my heart.

For the first time in forever, I hesitate a split second before strengthening the protection spell that will shield me from her magic. There's something very different about Aleah. She's an expert at hiding her conniving nature with something that looks authentic. I can't figure out what has set my senses on simmer, but suddenly I need to know more. Aleah's up to something with my brothers, I can feel it. I completely ignore the voice of logic telling me I'm letting my fear rule my brain. I'm simply not wired for emotional outburst. I stubbornly ignore the voice of my conscience calling me out for the liar I am.

Aleah is a knockout, smoking hot in the black dress I chose for her, and she's added black fingerless elbow gloves that she's pushed down to the wrist. I can feel the tension vibrating off her as she approaches. She's taking quick breaths, but her bright look tells me she's eager and curious. She's under the influence of Tristan's memory manipulation spell and shows no sign of recognition. Tristan's charm has effectively removed all memory of me, Atroyel and Tristan from her mind. Her vivid brown eyes are glued on mine as if she's memorizing every feature and cataloging it for future reference. She stops where I'm leaning against the mirrored wall and sticks out her right hand.

"Hi, I'm Aleah. Good to meet you." Her words are short and clipped, like those of a woman used to wielding power and control, and she's using a fake name. Yet, a shadow of insecurity flashes behind her brilliant eyes before she shields them. She wears a mask of ornate filigree that does nothing to hide her hypnotic beauty.

"Kneel before me." I chop out the order, my tone filled with command as I add the standard BDSM hand motion—my open hand moving down with fingers together.

Aleah hesitates a moment before dropping to her knees, her movements have a hint of awkwardness that confirms she's not used to this protocol. She stares at me a moment and that look sends streaks of lightning to my cock before dropping her gaze to the floor.

"That's right. You will not look at me unless I command you to." I pause for effect. She says nothing. Excellent. "Recite my rules."

"I must not look at you unless commanded. I must not speak unless given permission or to say a safe word. I must remember and obey your commands. I must respond vocally to specific requests." She pauses a moment. "Sir."

I take a moment to examine the petite woman before me. Round buttocks and small breasts with hard nipples that poke through the silk dress she's wearing. Nipples that beg for my attention, but that will have to wait. As I agreed when I took on this role play, my responsibility as an Acquired Taste Dom is to ensure her first experience doing a scene will leave her wanting more. *Wanting me.* I push the unwelcome thought away. This session is strictly business, and I have work to do.

"I want you to stand up and face me."

She's rigid as I slowly circle her, taking in this gorgeous woman. Her black curls dance around her face in loose tendrils. I reach for the hint of her scent as it drifts by and catch something floral, something tropical. Something subtle that makes me want to own this woman. At least for tonight.

Time to test just how compliant my wannabe sub is. I slide my hands down her arms before pulling down the zipper I'd only recently zipped up. But this time, I unzip halfway, allowing the dress to slide down, while allowing a finger to trace a line down her spine.

It's everything I can do to keep my hands from grasping her pert breasts as they fall free and bounce invitingly. She instinctively crosses her arms over her breasts before she catches herself and forces her arms to her side. Her timidity sends another bolt of electricity through my cock. I take moment to admire the large brown nipples before pulling the dress back in place.

"Sit." I point to the love seat facing the floor-to-ceiling one-way glass. "Keep your eyes trained on the window. Understood?"

The tension in her body shows that she's unsure whether she should speak. "When I ask a question, you may answer."

"Yes, Sir. I understand." Her contralto voice excites me. She keeps her eyes trained on the floor. But first things first. I refuse to work with an inexperienced sub without the assurance that she knows what she's getting into. If I do my job well, she'll focus on her answers and drop the defensive wall. As she watches a few scenes, her reactions will show me any remaining responses she's trying to hide.

As soon as she's seated, I shift my position to stand directly in front of her. "As this is your first kink experience, I need to understand what you're hoping to discover in this experience. You have permission to speak freely. Let's start with your preferred pet name. Do you have one?"

Her eyes widen in surprise, and she chews on her bottom lip, her eyes still fixed on a spot on the floor. *Good. She's compliant.* I bring my wayward mind back to attention. She's thinking, that's all.

"Look at me, Aleah. When I give a command, I expect instant obedience. Do you have a preferred pet name?" I put enough steel in my tone to let her know I mean business.

I'm watching for it, or I might have missed the blush that colors the shell of her ears. "No, Sir."

"What do your lovers call you?" I study her as another blush infuses her fair skin.

"Beauty or babe, mostly."

"I like little girl or baby girl."

She snorts as the words leave my mouth. I quirk an eyebrow in question. "Quite the oxymoron given my age," she says, "And I'm nobody's little. Little play is a hard limit for me."

It's not the first time Aleah has mentioned little play, one of my favorites, and I file that tidbit away for later consideration.

"Any more disparaging remarks about your physique will earn your ten strokes with the flat of my hand." I lay the spanking card on the table for all to see. After a lengthy discussion in our earlier meeting, Aleah had agreed to reduce her list of hard limits and use her safe words if we ventured into territory that makes her uncomfortable. Atroyel had explained that the memory manipulation spell would not make her do anything she wasn't already inclined to do. His reassurance had resulted in her moving a bunch of her *no-chance-in-hell options* to the *maybe-we'll-see category* giving me all the leeway I need.

She shifts a bit on the leather couch. This time the blush makes its way to her cheeks, staining them a red that complements the reddish-brown undertones in her black curls.

"Do you have any questions about my rules?" I ask. I'd included an explicit list of rules for Aleah to review before this scene, including to address me as Sir, keep her eyes respectfully lowered, and not to move or speak, unless to say her safe word. One the scene starts, I, as Dominant, will have complete control and expect full cooperation from the submissive.

"No, Sir," she replies quietly.

"BDSM play is all about a state of mind, which brings us to yours. Why are you here, little one?"

A fleeting smile catches the corners of her lips. Another blush reaches her ears as her eyes dart away from mine. *Little one* it is, then.

"That will be ten strokes for disobeying my command. Eyes on mine. Hiding your thoughts is not an option." I bark out the order, and her eyes shift back to mine. I cross my hands over my suit jacket and wait. While many choose to dress in fetish gear to attend an event, I prefer the power suit that clearly shows who is in control. First impressions, after all, make a huge difference in setting the right mood for the scene.

After several minutes of worrying her bottom lip while her eyes dance from mine and back to the floor again, she straightens her shoulders. "A friend of mine suggested you dominant types are better lovers, and I'm here to find out." Her eyes flash with a *there-I-said-it* look that sends another surge of blood straight to my cock. Her eyes drop to the tent in my trousers before darting back to mine.

"Are you hoping to become part of the lifestyle, or are you just a player?" A little test to see how far she's willing to go with this without the stumbling block of memories with Atroyel.

"Meaning?" This little angel is a thinker, not the usual sensation princesses who come to a club like this looking for a bit of fun with the rich and potentially famous.

"Meaning, are you hoping to get a taste of what it's like to live as a submissive twenty-four-seven, or are you merely looking for a bit of sexual titillation?

Her shudder gives me all the answer I need, but she says, "God no. There's not a chance in hell I'll let a man tell me what to do outside of the bedroom."

I hide a frown as she lets some of the pieces of her puzzle slip into place. The memory manipulation spell hasn't changed her story . . . at least not yet. She's only willing to concede control for sexual purposes, and she's not very experienced. I decide to test my theory.

"Where is your favorite place to have sex?"

A slight frown crosses her face as if she's worried her answer will disqualify her.

"There is no right or wrong answer, little one."

"I've only ever had sex on a bed, chair, or couch except for once in the shower, so I guess I'd have to say the bed." The expression on her face makes it clear she doesn't like announcing her inexperience. Almost as an afterthought, she adds, "I got fingered in an elevator once. That was fun."

I clamp down on the words "with whom" before they drop out of my mouth. There's not a chance that Atroyel groped anyone in an elevator. He'd die before making such a public display of himself.

"What was fun about it?"

She pauses a moment before answering. "His passion, I guess. He wanted me and couldn't wait to have me."

I quirk another small smile as she leaks that secret, revealing her need to be desired. "And did he?" I ask.

"Did he what?" She pauses a beat. "Have me? Yes. I guess you could call it that." She grimaces then smooths her features.

"Meaning?" A smile tugs at her lips as I toss her question back at her.

"Meaning he was a thirty-second wonder." She sucks in her lips as if trying to pull the words back.

6

CASSIEL

Aleah fills the silence that follows her comedic and rather pathetic description of a former lover by fidgeting with the hem of her dress. I use the moment to engage my mind probe and search her thoughts. Aleah's synapses fire like bullets from a semiautomatic machine gun, and her gaze bounces from my face to my crotch and back.

Shit. Fuck. What is wrong with you, girl? Guys hate to be reminded about their performance. Not that this guy looks like he's got performance issues. He's got a hard-on and a fuck-you attitude. What the fuck am I doing here? Have I lost my mind? He said he's going to spank me. Do I really want this? YES!!! NO!!! What if he hurts me? Great time to start worrying about that. You did ask for this. Could we get on with this, please? Fuck!

Her heart drums a staccato of excitement. "I meant to say he wasn't very good." She gives a *what-can-you-do* shrug.

"I'd much rather have a play partner's passion work on a slow burn. A partner whose willingness to please me shows the depth of their passion for me. Wouldn't you?" I let a smile play at the corners of my lips.

She bites her bottom lip.

"It's not a trick question, little one. You can relax. This is the getting to know you part of our evening."

She relaxes a bit, crossing her legs almost automatically before realizing I haven't instructed her to move. She quickly uncrosses them. "Sorry . . . um . . . Sir."

I ignore the slip for now. "What didn't you like about the shower?" I ask.

"I had to focus on too many things to concentrate."

"Concentrate on what?" Now we're getting closer to the root of what she truly seeks, I send a few more telepathic threads through her mind, and although there's still a brick wall in the back recesses of her mind, I don't sense any deception.

She takes a moment to consider her answer. "Perhaps concentrate is the wrong word. Distractions make it hard for me to relax." She stops as if there's more, but she'd prefer not to reveal it. I've heard enough to take her measure. It's not uncommon for those who wield power, personal and professional, to find focussing on nothing but the sex helps them stop the noise and take a break from the constant pressure to perform. Atroyel had chosen this roleplay well.

"What in particular would you like to try with me?"

"A blindfold and maybe beginner restraints. If, and only if, I can get out of them. And an orgasm." The last three words are a whisper.

Despite my best intentions to say detached, this woman continues to intrigue me. I decide to give myself a break and enjoy the moment. For the first time in forever, I want to prolong this encounter. I like that she doesn't pretend she doesn't know her mind. "What are you afraid of?"

"Nothing. In case of an emergency. You know, like if you had a coronary, and I need to save you." She gives me a persuasive smile, one that I'm sure she uses on her corporate victims. I say nothing for a few beats.

"Is there anything you'd like to add to the list of things you'd like to try?" In addition to soft bondage, she was curious about collars and following orders. And my mention of spanking had released the perfume of her wet hot scent. That gives me plenty of room to start with. "Do you remember my hard limit?"

She nods. "I am not to touch you without your permission." Her eyes sparkle as if now that I've mentioned it, it might be fun to try.

"Just to be crystal clear, little one, try it, and I'll spank your ass raw. Trust me when I say it won't be one of those sexy spankings that make you wiggle your ass under my hand and beg to be fucked."

"Got it." She looks as if she's about to roll her eyes, then thinks better of it. "And since I'm sure you're going to ask me about safe words next, I prefer the stoplight. Red for stop, yellow for carrying on but stop the intensity, and green for full speed ahead." She recites this line as if she's pulled it right out of one of the soft-porn romance novels.

"That's another ten strokes for speaking without permission."

Her mouth snaps shut, and she drops her gaze to the floor as another rush of heat rolls through her.

"Shall we begin?" I don't wait for her to answer. "Eyes forward. You're about to watch a scene. When it's done, I want you to tell me what you liked about it."

I'd decided to give Aleah a taste of what she'd experience at the kink event she'd be attending on Friday night. I open a portal to the club I'd chosen and step into a room that's identical to the one we left. Aleah follows me, looking around. I point to the large sofa facing the glass wall, and Aleah obediently perches on the edge of the seat.

The room on the other side of the glass is rectangular with a black rubber floor. Spaced throughout it are pieces of equipment: a St. Andrew's cross, a spanking bench, a regular wooden chair with no arms, and a padded table much like a massage table save for the fact that it's adjustable like a hospital gurney and has a groping hole in the middle. Play gear—floggers, restraints, and anything else you could need—hang on one wall.

A woman in a cage bra and black PVC pants with a zipper at the crotch stands before a seated man.

"You may approach," says the man.

She kneels in front of him, head bowed. "Sir, I'd like to explore breath play."

Aleah gives me a curious look following a sharp intake of breath. She's trying her best to give the image of calm, cool control, but her insides are dancing with excitement. I give her a nod of permission. *You may speak.*

"Breath play?" Aleah says, her brow furrowing.

I sit beside her and whisper in her ear. "Restricting a sub's breathing for a short period while sexually stimulating them can heighten arousal. It can also be very dangerous. Neck structures can easily be damaged, and too much time without oxygen can be deadly. But a hand over the mouth and a clear safety gesture for the sub can make it very hot."

As she'd described in their diary, she shivers and squeezes her legs together when my lips tickle her ear. I let her sit this way as we watch the Dom control the sub's breath while teasing her clit with his fingertip until she reaches an explosive orgasm.

Aleah sighs as the room darkens. The smell of her arousal almost makes me lightheaded. I tap her legs, and she parts them slightly. I rest my hand on her thigh. If she pretends she's not turned on, I'm prepared to make her prove it.

"What did you like?" I push her dress up and stroke a small area on her thigh, enjoying her soft skin.

"She sounded as if she was really enjoying it. Not like the

fake moaning in porn movies." She let another interesting nugget slip. "But I'd never try something so dangerous, not in this lifetime." She doesn't seem to be kink-shaming, merely making a statement of fact.

I pull her to her feet and lead her through an adjoining door to the next viewing room. The next sub asks to be edged by a dominatrix—masturbated but not allowed to come. The sub is an enormous man and dressed like a biker. Again, I have Aleah sit beside me and place my hand loosely on her thigh. She relaxes as she watches the scene unfold before us. She gives a similar answer when I debrief, but there's a damp spot on the couch, giving further evidence of her arousal.

In the scene, a woman with hair twirled into horns wearing a leather bustier and hot pants stands over the sub. He lies on the floor while she allows him to worship her feet by rubbing them on his face and licking her toes.

She walks a few feet away from him. "Strip and lie on the table," she says to the huge man. "You know where to put that cock of yours. Safe word, slave?"

"Red," the slave says over his beefy shoulder.

I watch Aleah's reaction. Her eyes widen as the Domme gracefully slips under the groping hole and teasingly drags her finger down the man's already purple cock.

"Oh, look," she says mockingly, catching precum on her finger. "You're already dripping." She rubs it onto his cock head and then takes her hand away. The slave's ass trembles on the table. She blows on the wet tip of his cock, and he groans. She pauses again and gives his crown a hard suck, making a popping sound when she lets go.

The slave's cock starts to twitch as if it's looking for its next touch. But the Domme doesn't touch it, making him groan again. Instead, she winks at the two-way glass as if aware we're her audience.

For several more minutes, she teases him before announcing, "Flip over. Let me see how needy your cock is." Her tone remains mocking but playful.

Panting, the slave lifts up and pulls back onto his knees to extract his cock.

"Faster!" the Domme says. "We didn't negotiate a spank, but you need one, don't you?"

The slave swiftly repositions himself on his back, and instantly, the Domme cranks the head of the table up, so he's sitting, legs out front.

"I want our guests to see me ruin your orgasm." She circles him, looking at his bobbing cock. Then she restrains his hands and feet at the sides of the table.

The expectant look on the sub's face has me gritting my teeth as if I'm experiencing the scene. Aleah's mouth hangs open, and her eyes are glassy. My little one leans forward, eagerly watching the action while trying to appear as if she's seen everything and nothing impresses her anymore.

The Domme gives the purple cock a long lick. The slave's breaths trip over each other. She wraps her hand around his girth, giving it a few pumps, and his hips thrust up into her hand, which she instantly snatches away to a very disappointed groan.

Walking to the back wall, she takes a moment to choose two toys: a leather crop and a vibrator. Back at the table, she holds up both, tilting her head. "Which to torture you with, beautiful slave?"

His eyes are wide.

She gives his cock a slap with the crop, and it bounces off his stomach and back up. His groan is shakier. She does this a few times, then pumps his shaft again before snatching her hand away. The slave gasps and moans as if his orgasm is imminent. But the Domme stands back and calmly observes his twitching cock.

"Look at you. You want to come *so badly*. Poor, poor slave."

Two painful minutes later, once his breathing has slowed down, she waggles the vibrator at him and holds it at the base of his cock where it meets his balls. She turns it on.

The slave grunts, his cock twitching, his body shaking, and then just as his hips rise off the table and it's obvious he's about to orgasm, the Domme laughs and removes the vibrator.

"Oh, my God."

I give Aleah a sharp look as she groans out the three words, but her attention is glued to the scene unfolding before us.

"Arrgh." The slave thuds the back of his head against the table. Semen weeps from his cock in weak little jets. No full-force release of orgasm for this boy, at least not yet.

"Now stay there so I can watch how long it takes you to go soft," the Domme says.

Aleah jerks in surprise, and I feel it as our thighs touch. "So, she's just going to leave him there like that?" She seems appalled as the Domme tortures the poor slave.

"She is, and he loves it. Now it's your turn." I stand and hold out my hand. Hesitantly, she puts her small hand in mine and lets me pull her to her feet.

7

CASSIEL

Aleah squares her shoulders but follows when I open up the portal taking us back to our island retreat. When she comes to a stop in the center of our playroom, she clasps her hands together and, with her head slightly bowed, looks at me and waits.

"Little one." I roll the pet name I gave her around in my mouth. "Your honest thoughts about the last scene. Did it appeal to you or turn you off, or both, and how?"

When she speaks, her voice is clear and confident. "I am new to this BDSM stuff, but I found that scene super hot. It turned me on because the slave gave his trust to his mistress to bring him to an excited but unsatisfied physical state, providing him with an experience that is a reward for him for psychological or physical reasons that are his own." She rushes over her words as she tries to hide her nervousness.

I'm impressed by her self-awareness but manage to hide my surprise at her insight. I berate myself and repeat my prime directive: find her dirty little secrets. Aleah's probably repeating something she read when she did all this research she talks about.

"And if this were a kink of yours, which role would you prefer to play? The Domme's, the slave's, or both?" I ask.

"The slave's," Aleah replies without hesitation. "As long as the Dom understood that I would like only teasing or taunting and not humiliation."

I move a step closer to her, invading her personal space. "Did you see how much pleasure the sub enjoyed despite the pain of having his genitals whipped? How did you feel watching? How would you feel about being treated like that?"

"I don't know."

She's not ready to let me know just how much the idea of being flogged excites her, but the rapid beat of her heart gives it away.

"Have you ever fantasized about being spanked?"

"Sometimes." She could barely get the word out. I look at her for a long beat.

"But?" Time to probe.

"My life has been predicated on being in control. When I think about my sexuality, my world gets turned upside down, and it frightens me. I fantasize about being dominated all the time. Part of me wants to explore this world of bondage and submission, and part of me is scared to death and wants to run and hide." Her blush deepens as she fidgets with her hands.

"Hide from what?" I push.

Inhibitions circle through her mind, but Tristan's memory manipulation spell removes the runway, so they can't land, freeing Aleah's natural reactions. Moral admonitions rush by too fast for me to read as I probe her mind. She's silent so long that I wonder if I lost her, but I force myself to stay still, to wait her out. Finally, the mental resistance drops away, and I'm left staring at the reality of what may be her biggest fear.

"I'm hiding from the true slut I am," she whispers. "I'm

afraid spreading my legs is the only thing I'm good for. I shouldn't like sex. Only bad girls like it."

I'm not prepared for the slide show of abuse that yawns open as Aleah answers my question. Each image details the horror she lived through, and her terror hits me with a solid right hook. I'd put a spell in place to protect me from any hidden agendas she might have, tricks she could play, but I hadn't thought about needing protection from what I learn about her. Or the effect it has on me. I shake the thoughts away and focus on the present, something I have to do with Aleah far too often. I have a job to do, and it's time to get it done.

"You're safe with me, you know. I won't push you further than you want to go."

"It's not you that I'm afraid of. It's me." She stops abruptly and pushes up her glasses.

I gaze at her and wait. Then, I run a finger over the goose bumps that appear on her arm.

"It's time to stop hiding, little one. Give me your glasses." I hold out my hand to her. "Are you ready to play?"

She hands me the glasses with tentative resolve, and I lead her into a room very much like the first playroom we'd seen. I keep my movements easy and controlled while I pick up an armless wooden chair and place it in a clear space. Standing in front of it, I crook my finger at her. Aleah shivers.

"We're negotiating the spanking scene," I say, and she nods. "Any additional hard limits?"

Aleah seems to consider this for a moment, then shakes her head. "Hands only. No canes or whips or anything."

I nod. "Is sexual touching permitted?" Fucking her hadn't been part of the plan, but that was before I'd watched her responses to the scenes and probed her mind. *You're making a mistake.* I push the warning voice of my conscience out of my head. I'd fucked countless women and walked away. There's no reason Aleah should be any different.

Aleah's breath comes out in a shudder. "Yes," she lets out in a rush of breath.

"Safe word?" For some reason, it's become my prime directive to make this the best sexual experience of her life. Better than anything my brothers have given her, and I want there to be no room for misunderstanding about consent.

"Red," she says.

"Strip."

Aleah's eyes widen into saucers. I cross my arms and tilt my head, expecting her to stop and renegotiate. But damn if she doesn't start taking off her sandals. She presents her back for me to undo the zipper yet again. I push it off her shoulders, and the silk pools around her ankles. I cross to the chair and sit while she folds her arms, shielding her naked breasts . . . or perhaps the stone-hard nipples screaming her desire.

"Good, little one." I pat my lap. "Now, come here."

If there's one thing I'm good at, it's my craft. I've run into skittish fillies before, and my appreciative murmurs and gaze turn Aleah's shyness into ease.

She walks her shapely body toward me as if there's no other place she'd rather be.

"Stop." I give her another thorough once-over. In response, she blushes and bites her lip.

I spread my thighs apart. "Now lie across my lap. Ass up."

Aleah slowly does as I command, and I hook my right arm under her collarbone to cradle her, sliding my other hand up her thighs and over the swell of her perfect ass. I take a minute, caressing and kneading her soft globes. And then, *smack*. I bring my hand down low on her ass, my hand spanning both cheeks, and then immediately soothe the spot tenderly.

Ignoring the precum leaking from my cock, I train every

sense on Aleah's emotions and see nothing but curiosity and desire. She doesn't make a sound.

I tap one ass cheek five times, each time with a little more force. Her small breasts jiggle seductively with every spank. The final crack makes her jump in my lap, one leg bending at the knee before straightening. I even her out by doing the same on the other side, but Aleah lets out a moan this time.

I slide into Dom space, that place of connection, concentration, and heightened senses, the moment she slips into subspace, showing she's totally immersed in the scene. I can't help it. Impact play is my favorite kind of kink. I run my hand gently up and down Aleah's smooth back, using my nails to gently scrape her, making goose bumps break out across her skin. I almost combust as I admire her rosy ass.

I land another thudding slap right where her ass meets the crease of her leg with a thump designed to vibrate right through her clit. And I'm right because Aleah moans without volume control and grinds her cunt against my thigh. *Delightful.*

Every so often, I let my fingers graze Aleah's entrance, gauging her arousal. Before long, the smacking, caressing, and kneading whips Aleah into a writhing, moaning, begging mess. "Please," she pants.

"Please, what?" I ask, my voice dripping liquid sex that's authentic for the first time in forever. All of my best intentions fly off into the horizon. I'm going to fuck this woman. My traitorous cock instantly rewards my false narrative that fucking her will purge her from my system.

"Please make me come, Sir." She says it without hesitation. As if she knows and trusts me.

"You ask so nicely." The hand cradling Aleah's upper body slides to graze her nipple, while the other teases her folds, making her ass wiggle. "You're eager, aren't you?"

"Yes," she whimpers.

"Well, since you've been a good little one, I'll give it to you right away."

"Thank you, Sir." She blurts the words out, the relief in her voice evident. I can't believe my ears.

Slowly but with rhythm, I twist three fingers inside her. I slide my other hand across her nipples gently, ever so gently, while I press hard into her cunt. Her body starts to shake, small unintelligible sounds coming from her mouth. She's right on the edge, about to erupt. I want this woman to have pleasure but want to deny her at the same time.

As I think that, I remember the prison fantasy from the diary. I press my thumb into the perfect rose of Aleah's asshole, and her body shudders and shakes, cries of pleasure falling from her lips as her orgasm hits her. Her blue-white grace rises from her skin like early morning mist over a meadow.

For several minutes, I soothe her with my hand, stroking her skin until she's ready to sit up. Then I sit her on my lap and cradle her, giving the appropriate psychological after-care. At least that's what I tell myself. Her eyes are closed, and her face wears a look of satisfaction and something else —surprise perhaps? She opens her eyes and gives me a grateful smile, and dammit, I do something I never do with subs. I brush my lips over hers, breaking another cardinal rule of no intimacy.

There's no mistaking the sexual chemistry that radiates between us, obviously a by-product of this intense shared experience. My competitive nature shifts into high gear. At least that's what I credit for this sudden surge of desire. I want to be the one to give Aleah the first breakthrough that will allow her to enjoy the full extent of her sexuality.

8

CASSIEL

Ignoring my best intentions, I pick Aleah up and toss her on the bed before binding her hands high above her head with a braided cord that matches the black silk blindfold I slide over her eyes. My breath catches as I gaze at her naked beauty. I'm completely in love with the splendor of her curves and the soft folds between her thighs just inviting me to lose myself in the rapture of her arousal.

After shedding my clothes, I stretch out beside her and trace my fingers around the curve of her ear. I lean over to kiss the slight dip at the base of her throat. My cock stiffens as she trembles in anticipation, and a deep rose blush highlights skin the color of fine desert sand she reminds me of. I ignore its insistence, intent on enjoying every second basking in her arousal.

I lick from the base of her neck to her right nipple and flick the engorged bud with my tongue, alternating with a slow circling of her areola. I caress the shapely globe in my hand, and her nipple stiffens in its cry for my attention. I answer the call, sucking the fullness of its nub deep into my mouth. She whimpers and arches her back. I relax the suction until she falls back on the bed. I plan to take my time with this little one. Now that I have her in my bed, I intend to make her mine . . . for the night. The logical part of my mind tries to push past this newfound emotion. With a mighty thrust, I lock it in a box for examination later . . . much later.

I worship each breast, each temple of temptation. Aleah cries for more, rolling and moaning in her urge to have me move to the epicenter of her desire. She struggles, letting her body scream her message. If her hands were free, I have no doubt she'd push my hand to the well of wetness hiding between her thighs. I trail a finger down the soft, smooth skin of her abdomen, content that I've made the right choice in binding her wrists to the headboard. I'm the teacher; she's the pupil. I'll give her sex like she's never experienced before.

I smell the perfume of her arousal as she writhes and begs for more. Using fingers and tongue, I pay homage to each part of her perfection—her cute little belly button, the gentle slope of her stomach, the curve of her waist. I inch my way down to her mound of Venus. I pause. Everything about her fills me with longing. For a split second, I'm envious of my brothers' claims on this woman who is so obviously made for pleasure.

I slide my finger over her mons into the slick folds of her labia. The head of her clitoris stands at attention, begging for another release. She widens her legs, unleashing the beautiful fragrant musk that's distinctly her own. I inhale deeply, sure I've never smelled anything so enticing, so fresh, so feminine. I gently part her full dark lips and gaze, stunned, at her sweet cleft. Again, I'm awestruck at the beauty of this woman who opens herself before me. I lean down and blow gently on her button of bliss. She rears up as if hit by another surge of electricity. I close my lips around her clit. A low, deep moan escapes her as she goes perfectly still.

As I torment, tantalize, and tease her with my tongue, her muscles start to vibrate with pent-up tension. Relentless in my enjoyment of her hunger, I take her to the edge of the cliff then bring her back. There. Back. There. Back. I lose track of how many times I tease her. I continue until she writhes, and moans, and groans, and I know there's nothing else in her world except for me and the sensations I pull from her. I clamp down on her pussy and suck with deep, long pulls, reveling in the taste of her exquisite nectar. She screams as release jolts through her, and she sinks, shuddering, onto the bed.

I stand, rubbing my fingers along the hard thickness of my shaft, giving myself one last beat before I submit to this moment. I bend and take one more long pull on each nipple, releasing another set of post-orgasmic tremors in her. Desire sweeps through me like a river rushing toward white water rapids, and my cock grows ever harder as it screams for attention. I plunge into her tight channel. My balls and anus tighten as the first familiar pulsing of release hits the base of my member. I still. I will make this last.

After an exceedingly long moment of sheer will, I get myself back under control. I inch my cock out of her, then slowly submerge. Nothing has ever felt better in my life, nothing. I grab a handful of her ass to help distract me from the pulsing demands my cock makes as it begs for its due. Aleah rocks her hips, matching my thrusts as her sheath tightens rhythmically around my singing shaft. Her petite body wakens one of my favorite fantasies. Red flags start waving madly in my mind as I make the split-second decision to see what happens if I push past her limits. After all, it's my job to find out how Aleah's triggers work, or so I tell the voice of my conscience. Caught up in a frenzy, I brush my five o'clock shadow against her cheek and murmur in her ear.

"Come for Daddy, baby girl."

Nothing in my extensive experience prepared me for her dramatic reaction. Every muscle in her body tenses to the verge of paralysis except for her head, which thrashes from side to side as she sobs out one repeated word, "No."

My head jerks up, and I search the room for some invisible threat before returning my gaze to Aleah's face. She's biting her upper lip and terror leaks from every pore. I cup her cheek, hoping my touch will reassure her. The instant our skin connects her back bows. She screams. Her eyes fly open, fixed on some distant enemy, and her breath escapes in sobbing gasps, but her bound wrists keep her from escaping.

"No, never again." As the scream leaves Aleah's lips, a massive blast of divine light slams me against the far wall.

9

ALEAH

Memory floods back when I wake cocooned between Troy and Tristan, a spot that's quickly becoming my happy place. I'd acted like a wanton slut, that I remember clearly. When it comes to my sex drive, shame is my first reaction. Fear follows quickly on the heels of shame as I peer into two sets of concerned eyes, examining me like I'm a lab specimen. The last thing I remember is a blinding white light and Cass's body flying across the room.

"What happened? Is Cass okay?" I try to sit up but meet the resistance of Troy's hands holding me in place.

"Oh, no you don't. Not until we make sure you're okay. Cass is just fine." There's a hard edge to Troy's tone that I can't quite identify.

Tristan lifts my arm and inspects it closely and not in a sexy way.

I resist the urge to yank my arm away. "Um, what are you looking for?"

"I'm making sure we healed all your burns," Tristan says.

Burns? What the fuck? "May I have my glasses please?" I no sooner ask, and Tristan's placing them in my open palm.

These magic powers of theirs sure come in handy. This time, Troy lets me sit up as I slide my glasses into place, but neither guy moves. I glance from one to the other, trying to figure out what's got them so worked up. My newfound spidey sense says Tristan is mad as hell while Troy is sad, resigned, and pissed.

"I'm fine. Why wouldn't I be? I feel better than I have in a long time." The weird tingling in my extremities reminds me I haven't taken my medication. By the looks of the blazing sun dancing with cloud ribbons high in the sky, it's at least noon, but first things first. "What happened? What's wrong?"

"First, your pills, then we talk." Troy hands me one of my small medicine cups, holding my cocktail of minerals and prescription meds along with a small glass of orange juice. He knows I have trouble taking pills with water, and I give him a grateful smile appreciating his thoughtfulness. I swallow the fistful of tablets and down the juice giving a happy sigh as the sugar hits my system. Troy takes the empty glass and sets it on the bedside table.

"There. Now, are you guys going to tell me what's wrong?" I push up my glasses and run my hands through my hair, although there's not much I'll be able to do with my unruly curls without a comb and styling gel. I ignore the slight soreness between my legs that reminds me of last night's activities and focus my attention on my guys.

"How are you feeling?" Tristan asks. "How much do you remember about what happened last night?"

I frown at the two of them; I know with all their hovering, they're hiding something. "I'm feeling fine. I've got a bit of a headache and that weird tingling numbness I sometimes get, and I'm starving, but otherwise, I'm fine. And I remember everything up until the big bright light. Speaking of bright light, where is Cass?" I vaguely remember watching

Cass fly across the room when the bright light appeared. Maybe it's an angelic thing.

Both of them nod but say nothing. Tristan passes his open palm over me. I send a silent prayer to the gods for patience and take a deep breath.

"So," I drag the syllable out, "what happened next? Was the bright light from Cass's power? Why aren't you two answering my questions?" I turn to Troy, who gives a little shrug.

"We thought it best to keep you two apart," he says. "From what we can piece together, something he said or did activated your power, and you blasted him with divine light."

"What do you mean I blasted him with divine light? Is he okay? And what the fuck is divine light?" My heart hammers into overdrive, although I'm not sure why. I pull the sheet under my arms to cover my naked body and scamper to the end so I can climb over the guys. If they don't tell me what's going on, I'll find out for myself. This time, it's Tristan who pushes me back.

"Let's slow down and take a minute, Ali. What's happening is new to all of us. Cass is fine, although a bit battered and bruised."

"He'll live, and that's more than he deserves," Troy grumbles. It's not like him to make judgments on others unless he thinks they're a threat to me. Otherwise, Troy could give a shit how others behave. Or he's trying to distract me. I narrow my eyes at him.

"How did Cass get battered and bruised?" Oh yes, investigative journalist Aleah has just come out to play.

"You blasted him with a divine light strike," Tristan says, "and it was powerful enough to knock him out and burn your arms." I follow his gaze as it returns to my arm. There's no hint of any burns.

"And what, pray tell, is a divine light strike?" My tone is

pointed and edgier than I mean to sound, but I want answers. When Troy is in one of his moody states, answers would be like pulling impacted teeth.

"It would appear that the gods gifted you with the ability to create, shape, and manipulate light and energy from the heavens. As far as we knew, only superior angels, such as archangels or angel lords, possess the ability to create divine light. In truth, the Nephilim were such a threat to demonic power they were eradicated, and their history is the stuff of ancient history, so we don't know much about your power," Tristan says. "The burns are probably a result of not knowing how to control your power."

"We do know the gods are very eager to help you come into your powers because you're strong enough to kill a demon lord. Troy's words are measured, and his sadness almost brings tears.

"Okay, so why are you so sad," I look over at Tristan, "and you so mad?" I'm not beating around the bushes any longer. I want answers.

"Cass stepped over a line." Troy's tone tells me I'm not going to get more out of him until he's good and ready. I look back and forth, trying to figure out what the fuck Cass could have done to elicit this depth of emotion. Why aren't they pissed at me for injuring their brother?

"I get that, but what did he *do* exactly?" I can't let it go.

"Why don't you tell us what he did, babe?" Tristan brushes some of my hair behind my ear, and for a split second, all I want to do is cuddle up and lean into his touch. Instead, I sigh and put on my self-examination hat.

"I'm pretty sure you two with your telepathic connection are well aware of what we were doing." I pause to see if Troy will take the bait I throw him. If he does, I'll know whatever is bugging them isn't all that bad. I look over at him, but his head rests against the headboard with eyes closed. There's no hint of a smile or request for me to provide the salacious details, just sadness similar to when he was dying. Whatever he thinks Cass did, it's serious. I close my eyes and go inside my head, prying loose the moment I'm trying to avoid recalling. A crystal-clear image appears as the curtain shielding the memory parts. *Oh, shit.* I've gone and done it again, caused a rift between Troy and his family. *Fuck! Fuck! Fuck!* I open my eyes and rotate my head to relieve some of the tension building in my traps as shame and embarrassment build in me. Why does shit like this always happen to me? That's right, Aleah, hop right on down pity party lane.

"He didn't do anything really." Praying I don't sound as lame as I feel. "I felt a man's whiskers on my face at the same time as he said, "Come for daddy, baby girl," I choke out. "I remember screaming for him to stop in my mind, so that must have triggered what you call a divine light strike. You can't blame Cass for the way my mind works. Sounds to me like he did his job pretty damn well since he activated one of my triggers." Clearly, there's something I'm missing here.

"I can and do blame him," Troy says. "We're going to have this out once and for all. I might be able to forgive Cass for ignoring the warning signs he saw in your mind in the name of protecting you, but he put his own selfish needs above yours by violating your hard limit of no littles play. That's not only unprofessional. It's unforgivable." He throws back the sheet and rapidly pulls on boxer briefs and jeans. It's damned near impossible to change Troy's mind once he gets a hate on for someone. "I'll get Cass and meet you both on the upper deck."

I can't help but follow that cute ass out the door. I'm not sure what's got his dander up so much, but I'm about to find out. I don't have a sense of me being any part of the problem, so I'm taking a back seat and seeing if I can figure out the dynamics between these guys. I haven't had much chance to see Troy with family, and I can't wait to find out more. Also, I need to get the story that's been percolating in my mind on paper, figuratively speaking.

"Having your hard limit violated must have been hard for you. How are you feeling, *mon chou*? Are you in pain?" Tristan's tone is empathetic, caressing. He traces a finger over our mating brand and gives me a smile that melts in my heart. But I've got to stop Troy before he does something he'll regret.

"I'm fine and beginning to wonder what all this fuss is about." I start to get off the bed, but Tristan pulls me into his arms. And earns a frown for it. Now is not the time.

"I get why thinking he might lose the relationship with Cass makes Troy feel sad, but what's got your cock in such a knot." That comes out with more of a bite than I intended, but all the negative energy coming from these two brings on another sick headache.

"I have the same problem as Troy. Cass stepped over a line even the most inexperienced sex angel knows better than to cross. "He violated one of your hard limits. He lost control." Tristan lacks the same forgiveness gene as Troy. They're very serious about this hard limit stuff.

"Look, I know you guys have your rules, but don't you think you're overreacting here? We agreed his job is to expose my triggers, right? And now you're both pissed that he did?" My righteous indignation raises my voice at least half an octave.

Tristan's frown remains in place. His lips part, and I rush to cut him off at the pass. "And you know bloody well what I'm feeling but if you're trying to see how self-aware I am, let's see, I don't understand why you two are so mad at Cass when I'm not, and I'm the injured party here. Last night triggered something that might be another of those pivotal growth moments, and I want to grab my laptop and get my thoughts out. And then I want you two to help me figure out what's happening inside me." I punch my chest. "And then, maybe, if I'm lucky, one or both of you will seduce me. *Bloody hell!*" The Canadian in me comes out full throttle as my ire rises.

Tristan's stern visage softens a bit, and a slight smile tugs at the edges of those very sexy lips. "We can still do all of that, *mon chou*, after we settle things with Cass."

Now it's Tristan who gets off the bed and throws on a pair of jeans and a T-shirt, bringing my avoidance tactics to an abrupt halt. I have to face Cass before I have time to figure out how I feel about what I experienced last night. And even worse, I'm going to have to referee one of Troy's walk-away moments when he throws down the gauntlet with Cass. I shrug on shorts and a T-shirt and try to formulate a plan. How the fuck does one confront a guy who'd made you come at least twice and hates your guts? I haven't been this conflicted since the first time Troy and I fucked and then pretended nothing at all had happened.

10

TRISTAN

I try to keep my temper under control as I walk through tension so thick you'd need a machete to cut through it. Whatever passed between Cass and Troy before I arrive has deepened Troy's grief. He's gone inside himself and doesn't acknowledge my existence. Cass is barely keeping a rein on guilt but fixes me with one of his aggressor stares. I turn my back on him, prepare two matcha green lattes, and set them on the table. When I'm ready, I look directly at him. He stares back but says nothing.

"I ought to punch you," I say. Not a great way to start, but my diplomacy takes a hike when I'm pissed. Troy is much better at handling Cass's alpha attitude.

"Go ahead," Cass says.

"Yeah, you'd like that, wouldn't you? So you can soothe your guilt with the sweet taste of victory or the sting of defeat. Well, it's not going to work, not this time." At my acid tone, Cass clenched his jaw; no doubt he is surprised by this confrontation from me. I'm a bit surprised myself, but I attribute the change to my angelic mating bond. The loose gears of my life are finally shifting into place, awakening emotions I didn't know were within my grasp. Protecting Aleah from assholes, even if one of them is my brother, just became one of my top priorities right after getting to know and loving her.

Aleah walks across the deck and slides onto the bench beside me. She's fighting another one of her mating connection headaches, but I force out a tight smile of reassurance as I hand her the latte. She gives me a wan smile of thanks but says nothing. Between sips, she sends furtive glances at Cass. No doubt his asswipe behavior is what's upsetting her, although, given her defense of his transgressions, I'm not sure what.

When Troy raises his head, his gaze goes directly to Aleah. They stare at each other for a long moment, but I can't sense anything beyond their deep and abiding love. Something flashes in his eyes, and he clears his throat. "Now that we're all here, we can get down to business." The hard edge of his gaze cuts through Cass's defensive shield as Troy lets his anger blow through that blanket of horrible sadness.

"Cass, you know the thing that pisses me off the most is your refusal to admit you've done anything wrong. Your reckless behavior could have gotten Aleah killed. She was covered in burns, for the gods' sake." Troy takes a deep centering breath as his intensity builds. "You're jeopardizing our status as sex angel lords, and for what? I told you not to push me, Cassiel. I begged you not to make me choose." Despite Troy's calm, controlled tone, his power makes each word an arrow piercing through Cass's armor.

It's clear Cass is going to use aggression as his protection from the guilt he feels. "What exactly did I do that's so wrong from your perspective, Atroyel? Tell me that. I did what we planned on having me do. I tested her limits and exposed a huge breach in her defensive wall. You should be thanking me for a job well done." Cass pours a dung heap of anger into his words, but for once, it doesn't affect me . . . at least not the way he wants.

I slip an arm around Aleah's shoulders and pull her into my side as we observe the fencing match. She stiffens for a second, then gives my heart and cock a tug as she snuggles against me.

"You were going to probe for triggers, not make a frontal assault without any support from your flank." Troy parries back. "Instead, you used your reality-warping power to interfere with our connection with her. You know the rules. We use that power only when extreme circumstances warrant it, and we all agree it's necessary. Are you trying to get yourself cast down?"

"Of course not," Cass retorts hotly. "I was trying to do my job without interference from two lovesick puppies. You neglected to tell me I was dealing with damaged goods."

They have another glare-down, and Troy's ice-cold temper clashes with the flames of Cass's defensiveness. Aleah stirs beside me but keeps her gaze focused on the action. I get the sense that she's not happy about being referred to as damaged, but it's as if there's static blocking the connection between us.

"What damaged goods are you referring to?" Troy's tone drops from frosty to glacial.

"Don't pretend you don't know the shit I saw in her mind. You should have warned me she has sexual, emotional, and physical triggers. Fuck, she's got so many, I don't even know what triggered her," Cass says.

Aleah straightens. Troy keeps his gaze on Cass, but his message comes through loud and clear. *Not yet, beauty. You'll get your turn.*

"Spare me your self-pity. Even the most inexperienced sex angel knows better than to trigger a breakdown," Troy says.

"So, what are you suggesting I should have done? Stop the scene and bring her out of subspace?" Cass asks.

"I'm strongly suggesting you take responsibility for your actions before you do something irreparable, Cassiel. Regardless of whether she said to proceed, you're a sex angel lord and subject to the laws that govern us. You know your job better than I do, so you'd better figure out what it is about Aleah or our mating bond that bothers you so much. I can put the lie about spanking without consent being part of our job down to exaggeration in the heat of the moment, but ignoring what you saw in her mind is strike two and a breach of trust. Violating a hard limit is unforgivable." Troy delivers a near-fatal blow in that way he has with words.

After another hot stare down, Cass drops his gaze.

"Okay, fine, you win. I gave into temptation. Sue me. It's not like one of you hasn't gone off half-cocked before. But what bothers me the most is that you two are so blinded by your cocks that you can't see what's in front of your face. This woman"—Cass stabs a finger in Aleah's direction—"is hiding something. I saw it in her mind. And that *something* has something to do with dismantling our unit. You know as well as I do that it's my job to neutralize any threats."

"My wife is not a threat, nor is it your job to neutralize her." The razor-sharp edge to Troy's voice cuts, each word removing an inch of flesh.

Aleah shrugs my arm off, stands and grabs her journal from the table. Clutching it to her chest, she turns toward my battling brothers. She puts a tight lid on her emotions, but only after I catch a glimpse of hurt feelings. "Excuse me, gentlemen. You don't need me here, and I need to get started on my article, but I want to say something first. This arrangement with the four of us living together isn't working. I think it's best if you keep your work life separate from my relationship with you." She looks at Troy and cracks her lips in the facsimile of a smile. "You're not going to be happy about my decision, but I've decided to go home after the event tomorrow. You can use your magic to protect me there, and that way, I won't be subjecting anyone to my presence."

"But—" Troy barely gets the word out before she cuts him off.

"No buts, Troy. I'll say this once, and then we'll never speak of it again. I'm done with trying to gain the approval of either of your families." Aleah's tears well up but stay firmly in place. Time enough later to admire her strength of will.

"I spent almost twenty years trying to get your family to accept me. When your mother told me I wasn't who she'd pick for her favorite son, I pretended it didn't matter. But it hurt like hell. As did the many comments about how 'odd' and 'different' I am." Aleah loses the battle, and she swipes at the tears running down her cheeks. "And you know I reached my ping point when they accused me of keeping you from them last year when you were dying, and I stopped trying to get their approval. I finally learned the lessons you tried so hard to teach me." Her gaze drifts over to Cass as she brushes away more tears and sniffs. Troy's emotional discomfort rises with each tear that falls. From what he'd told us, Ali doesn't cry often, and when she does, she's in severe distress.

I conjure a few tissues and hand them to her. She blows her nose and sighs. "I can't force you to like me, and I'm not going to fight a losing battle. I'm assuming we don't need to live together for you guys to work together. If going home makes it easier for the mirror's eye to find me, I'll take my chances. No hard feelings. I'll leave you to figure it out. I know you guys are all concerned about me and want to debrief, but first, I've got to write. Then, I can talk. That's part of my process. Carry on without me." She turns and walks off the deck, giving us a royal wave as she departs, acting all casual and shit. I want to appreciate her legs and ass, but I'm battered by the strength of the emotion she internalized. Despite the tears, she'd laid out her case with calm precision, and if it hadn't been for our bond, I wouldn't have guessed she hid a well of hurt and rejection.

The sounds of nature are the only thing that breaks the heavy silence between us for several long minutes. Troy sits with his head in hands fisted at his temples. Cass vibrates with impatience, but he knows better than to push Troy when he's in protective mode unless he wants his head taken off. Finally, Troy sighs and scrubs his face with his palms before looking at me with resignation in his eyes. Then Cass takes center stage in the spotlight of Troy's gaze. I'm fascinated by this new side of Troy. At the sign of the slightest emotional distress, I'm told Troy would have retreated so far into himself he'd be almost catatonic. The only exception to that had been when he had defended Aleah against Cass's wrath in the forest. Like then, his need to protect her gives him the strength to face his emotional demons. At those times, he became professorial as he tried to move Cass to see things the "right" way.

"I'm very disappointed in your behavior, brother. But I'm not here to lecture you. I've learned a lot about myself from Aleah over the years, particularly when I was dying. The depth of her love caused me to see things in a way I hadn't before, and I thank the gods for this second chance to truly accept her gift in a way I wasn't able to earlier. From the moment the doctor gave the terminal diagnosis, Aleah's strength, courage, and comfort were gifts I didn't deserve. She didn't try to run, hide, or try to cheer me up. Instead, she enfolded me in her arms and gave me the gift of my life." Troy stops for a moment and takes a calming breath as he stops himself from being overwhelmed by déjà vu. My heart hitches for a moment, and I'm not sure if it's with fear or joy.

If Aleah's love had brought about this transformation in Troy, what lies ahead for me?

"She offered to lay bare her soul and walk with me into the jaws of death, fighting until she had to let go if I'd let her. As tears of empathy streamed down her beautiful face, she'd asked me if I'd do the same. To do this, we both had to agree to be honest about what we were feeling. She made me promise I wouldn't try to shield her and promised to do the same." Troy pauses again, and I have to stop myself from bolting from the deck to find my salvation with Aleah.

"She chose to love me every single day. It was her strength, courage, commitment, and love that brought me through those horrendous years while she fought like a mother cougar to protect my process. She made sure I died with grace and dignity, putting my needs over hers too many times. It was and will remain the single most unselfish act of love I'll ever experience, and that includes my feelings for you. You can thank the gods that Aleah taught me to be a better person, Cass. Otherwise, I'd walk away right now. By my count, you're at strike three." Troy gives a tight smile. "And lucky for you, Aleah believes in forgiveness and second chances. So, you've got two strikes and three balls. Don't strike out."

Troy stands and opens his mind to me in that particular way we've had since childhood letting me know he's rubbed raw and needs some time to recharge before he can take the force of Aleah's emotions. Flying off to one of the uninhabited out islands will give him enough space from the strength of the bond.

"I need some time," he says unnecessarily.

I nod. "I've got this." He, in turn, senses my need to be there for him and Aleah and share some of this burden. He puts a reassuring hand on my shoulder for several seconds before spreading his wings and taking flight.

11

TRISTAN

I use my connection with Aleah like a tracking device and locate her sitting in a gazebo tucked amongst the palm trees on the private sandy beach surrounding our villa. Despite the darkened glasses shielding her eyes, it's clear she's been crying. I drop her laptop on the low table between the two lounge chairs occupying the shaded space. Sitting on the empty lounger, I pour us each a glass of fresh-squeezed lemonade from the frosted pitcher and offer her a glass.

Aleah takes several long swigs, ignoring my scrutiny as I try to get a read on the source of her upset. But she's guarding her feelings, although I get the sense it's out of concern for Troy and me. I stretch out and relax, watching a couple of Mediterranean gulls play hunt-and-peck at the water's edge, fighting the blast of her nausea and head pain that flows though our empathic connection. I wish I could heal her completely, but something is blocking my magic. It's her move, and I need to suppress my impatience and wait.

"Would you mind getting my pills, Tristan? It looks like I'm not going to beat this one on my own." Ali's voice is low but firm, with no sign of the physical distress she's suffering.

"I could do that, or I could do even better. I can heal you. All it takes is one kiss." I sit up and swivel so I can see her. She doesn't react for so long. I begin to wonder if she heard me. Just as I'm about to speak, she says, "Then what the fuck are we waiting for?" Her dry humor thread filters through to the spot in my chest that now houses part of her heart. With a grimace, she slides over so I can join her. I stretch out beside her and pull her into my arms. With a heavy sigh, she settles against me. I reach my healing power looking for the extra boost I'll need to heal bodily damage not caused by sex or using sexual energy.

As the healing grace starts to flow from me, I give a quick prayer to the gods and lower my lips to hers. At first touch, she's a passive participant as she absorbs my healing grace. We both relax into the kiss as desire replaces dissipating nausea and headache. She slings her legs over mine and grabs a handful of my hair as her kiss becomes a full-body activity, one that damned near takes me from this world to the next.

Our need for air breaks us apart, leaving us panting. Aleah tosses her now smudged glasses onto the table and props herself on an elbow as fire and heat dance in the flecks of her honey-amber eyes. She places a small hand over the place in my chest that protects her heart, and brilliant sunshine bursts through as her smile illuminates her face. The power of my love for this woman hits me like a physical force scaring the hell out of me and taking me to the pinnacle of joy in equal measures. She pats my chest and pushes herself to a sitting position.

"I believe I owed you that one." Her grin dies as another thought hits her. "Thank you for healing my headache. Are you okay?"

I cradle my head in one hand and stroke her arm with my free hand. "Yes, I'm fine. Why wouldn't I be?"

"I thought the act of healing emptied your reserves or whatever it's called. Last time, you guys had to run off to recharge." Her brow furrows as she closes her eyes, but she leaves her hand on my chest. After a minute or so, she lifts her hands. "You feel a little tired, that's all."

I put a lid on the excitement that leaps through as I realize what's happening. "What does that mean, I feel a little tired?"

Her ears turn red, and she refreshes our drinks as a distraction. But not before I realize it's shame, not embarrassment, causing the reaction.

"I know, it sounds weird." She laughs, but it doesn't hide her awkwardness. "I get feelings when I'm around people who are sick. It's like I can feel part of their pain or that something in their machinery is broken. The connection is powerful with Troy, and sometimes it takes everything I have to stay strong. Not that I'm complaining." She pushes her glasses on. "And now I can feel you."

Ali lifts the laptop and moves over to her chair, all business. "I don't mean to be rude, and I know you want to talk, but I need to draft this article while the experience is still fresh. Do you mind?" She grips the sides of the laptop as if preparing to defend her position. There's so much I want to find out about what makes this woman tick, and we have time.

"Do what you have to do, babe." I pick up the diary I'd brought along and open it to where I'd left off. "I'll catch up with what I missed in your Double Diary while I recharge."

Her smile is a warm blanket of love and gratitude as she opens her laptop. Within a minute, she's typing furiously and alternating between biting her bottom lip and muttering to herself. Like me, she seems to have the ability to focus her thoughts on drafting her article. My eyes drift closed as I block out everything else but being here with her at this moment.

"How do you guys describe your junk when you're losing your erection? Soft? Semi-soft?" Ali's husky contralto brings me back from the wet dream tickling at my resting brain. I crack my eyes open and lift my sunglasses. Instant alarm fills her as our eyes meet.

"In what context?" I keep my voice calm, hiding just how pleased I am that she's asking my opinion.

She fiddles with her laptop then passes it to me. "I've highlighted the sentence for you. What word would you use where I've written soft?" She sits up and swings her legs to the floor, focusing her attention on me.

"Now stay there so I can watch how long it takes you to shrivel," the Domme says.

I let out a chuckle as I pass the computer back to her. "Well, I certainly wouldn't use shrivel." I pause to make sure she's responding to my humor.

She grins back. "Have you ever seen what happens?" She holds her right index finger straight up, then slowly bends it toward her palm. "Yup, looks like it shrivels to me."

We both laugh as she sits back on her chair. "Don't distract me. I'm almost done."

"I wouldn't dream of it under one condition," I say.

She raises an eyebrow and waits for me to go on.

"You let me read your piece when it's done." I'm eager to learn everything I can about this woman, and I suspect the article will be as informative as the diaries.

She gifts me with another of those smiles that transform her face as delight washes through her. "Only if you agree to give me your honest opinion. Troy used to be my collaborator, but he lost interest when he got sick." She looks down at her computer while her mind does another mini analysis of what she's just said. "Not that I blame him. I'm not being critical, just analytical."

"I wouldn't have assumed otherwise," I say. My Ali acts as if she's been repeatedly criticized for falling short of someone's expectations. "Why do you second-guess most of your actions?" I give her a warm smile. "I'm not being critical, just analytical."

Her look of surprise turns to a smile as she accepts my jest for what it is. "I've gotten used to people misinterpreting or plain disapproving of my behavior, and I've worked very hard to be aware of when and where I do things that will piss people off."

"Ah. I see." I'll show her what we see of her—strong, loving, fiercely protective, empathic, and so much more. For now, I hold my peace so she can get back to her writing, and after a penetrating look, she does just that.

I return to reading the diary, sinking into the depth of Troy's emotion. The power in his poem hits me like a hard blow to the gut. "As apprehension faded to trust, a cool sweetness settled over us."

A warm glow fills me as I get the answer to a question I hadn't known to ask. Doubt about our angelic mating bond, or more specifically, my role in our union niggled at the back of my brain. After all, what, besides good looks did I have to offer Aleah? Troy had given her everything she needs, or so I'd believed. But I'm beginning to understand that she needs me to help her believe what Troy and I know.

I startle awake by the sound of Ali's laptop snapping shut. "Done." She gives a fist pump and a huge smile. I hold out my hand for the computer. Ali laughs as she opens the lid. "I'd hoped you'd forgotten."

"Not in this lifetime, *mon chou*. Don't worry; I'm not here to judge," I say.

"I'm just kidding. I'd love your feedback, but it will drive me nuts to wait, so I'm going for a short walk." She grabs the wide-brimmed hat she takes with her everywhere. "I won't be long. "It's late enough that I won't be burnt to a crisp."

"That's something else I can help with." I place a sunblock charm that will protect her sensitive skin from the sub-tropical sun. "Don't be long. I have the feeling Troy has something special planned for you tonight.

12

ALEAH

The sun is sinking into the horizon, lighting the skies with shades of blue that remind me of the three guys. Troy sits on my chair facing Tristan as I approach my gazebo hideaway, watching my guys' animated talk punctuated with waving arms. I can't tell what they're talking about, but whatever it is has them both rather excited. My dread meter rises, and I drag my feet just a bit, preparing for the inevitable criticism of my writing. While I welcome it and know it will push me to better work, just once, I'd love to have my work critiqued from the pretty-darned-good perspective.

Time to armor up and raise my shields so I can face the music. I push my glasses up the bridge of my nose and sweep loose curls behind my left ear. I repeat the action on the right side for good measure. With two of them going at me, I'll need the computer portion of my brain running on all cylinders to avoid an emotional reaction. I refuse to be the emotionally needy person my foster father accused me of daily. Which was a complete contradiction to the other daily mantra: you're so hard to like, no one will ever love you, and you're not capable of love. My logical brain and Troy's love helped me recognize the lie fueling my foster father's war on my self-esteem, but sometimes it takes a while for my heart to catch up.

Troy's intense tone lets me know he's in full-tilt debate mode before I can hear what he's saying. *Shit.* My heart sinks to its go-to first-reaction place—he hates the article. I pull myself back from the edge. *You don't have enough information to make that assumption.*

"It's plain as day if you look at what she says here." Troy points to something on my computer screen. "Look at his hard limit." He swipes at the keyboard. "And see here, he stops himself from kissing her. I'm telling you, he'd only do that if he felt vulnerable, exposed."

"I don't know, bro. He's never been the touchy-feely type, and he isn't sensitive to emotional assault. That's why he makes such a good warrior. He's ruthless." Tristan sounds more thoughtful than doubtful as I approach.

Troy pats the chair beside him and gives me a quick smile. I drop down beside him, accepting his unspoken invitation to join the conversation. One of the many things I know about this man is that he values my opinion as much as I do his. I rest a hand on his thigh, loving the increase in the warm hum that signals our connection. He wraps his fingers around mine. Touching him is like opening a shortwave radio channel on a frequency that only works for the two of us.

"We're talking about a theory I have. I think we've been going about this problem with Cass all wrong, beauty. As you no doubt gathered, Tristan disagrees with me," Troy says.

Tristan leans forward, forearms on thighs, and flashes me that delicious smile of his. "It's not that I disagree. I'm just not convinced Cass has this sensitive side," Tristan retorts.

"So, you get to help me get him to see the light." Troy squeezes my hand as he winks. He'll argue passionately for hours to persuade someone to see things his way, but he remained open to considering a logical argument.

I give him a *yeah-right* smile before reaching over and plucking an olive from the tray on the table. "Let's see if you can persuade me, and then we'll see who I'm helping, so hit me. Tristan, you go first because once Troy and I go at it, we might roll right over you." I smile, hoping he can see he's important to me, to us.

"Inadvertently, of course," Tristan says. His return smile lets me know he gets my message.

"Of course," I say.

"Troy thinks Cass is also your destined mate. I think opening himself to all this love is clouding his assessment of the situation," Tristan says. "He was supporting his argument with parts of your article. We disagree on the depth of Cass's emotions."

"I used to think the same thing," Troy says, "but now that the blinders are off, I see that Cass suffers from a lot of the same fears and insecurities that I did when it comes to love."

I snort. I can't help myself. "Duh. On steroids."

"So, what's your take on Cass?" Tristan asks. He's guarded, and I can't get a good read on him. I reach my free hand out to him. The instant our skin connects, our channel opens on its frequency, its own warm hum. He's battling his demons when it comes to Cass, and navigating that minefield will take a whole lot of empathy. I squeeze Troy's hand to tell him to shut the fuck up. He whooshes out a breath but subsides to a simmer.

"You've probably figured out by now that I work out a lot of things by writing," I begin.

Troy groans. "Oh gods, do we have to take a trip down memory lane to get to the point?"

"This is my story, and I'll tell it the way I want," I retort. Troy and I repeat a long-standing joke between us. In the early days, the way I'd communicated had been a source of contention between the two of us, but we'd worked through that ages ago as we came to appreciate each other as separate human beings. And now I get to figure out how angels work.

Tristan relaxes a bit, just as I'd hoped he would. "I'm with you, babe."

I give Troy an *as-I-was-saying* look and ignore the image of him sticking his tongue out. Now wasn't the time for playing around. "I wrote the article from the male point of view so I could try to put myself in the Dom's shoes, in this case, Cass's. One of the things that fascinates me about sex is the psychology behind it." I offer this for Tristan's benefit. Troy nods impatiently. *Get on with it, beauty.* I love this mental channel between us. *Time to explore that later.*

"To help develop the Dom character, I thought about the ways I have a similar emotional experience and realized we have a lot in common."

This time Troy snorts but stills when I give him "the look."

"Do elaborate," Tristan says rather dryly.

"From what I can gather from your childhood, your parents were fighting then killed in some great war, and Cass took on being the caregiver and making sure you two were taken care of. I did the same thing with my foster brothers and sisters. My foster mother was mentally ill, and you know about *him*." I take a beat to make the mental spit purge at the thought of my foster father. I love it when I see women do it in movies to show their contempt, although I'd *never* do something that gross in real life.

Tristan, however, has no such compunction because he makes a dramatic spitting sound in response to my thought. Troy squeezes my hand, partly in empathy and partly with impatience.

"Becoming a caregiver at an early age does a lot to mold

our character, especially someone as emotionally intense as you three. If my experience is any indication, Cass may be strangled by a few life lies that developed."

"Such as?" Troy asks. He leans forward and snags an olive and feeds it to me. Tristan lets go of my hand and puts a square of cheese between my lips. Their knees touch mine, keeping our connection channels open.

I explain between mouthfuls. "Things like adults can't be trusted to help, wanting things for myself is selfish and counter-productive, and emotions are pointless and get in the way." I lean forward and pour a glass of red wine, giving a silent prayer of appreciation for this resort's service.

"Prepare for a trip into the twilight zone." Troy's comment gets him another look. "She'll probably try to convince us that Cass will find love if we reveal his inner longing to dance on stage with Bruno Mars. And then she'll try to convince us that she can make that happen if she puts her mind to it."

I poke Troy's arm. "It was Prince, and now that he's dead, it's Bruno Mars. Now, back to Cass. He's sublimated his emotional needs into making sure his emotionally crippled brothers, no offense, have food and a roof over their heads. He has to keep them safe at all costs, especially when they're sent to apprentice with the sex lords, and that means he has to use his wits, not his heart. Cass rationalized his guilt whenever he's wanted something of his own, but now he's about to lose his reason for living.

"Troy said something when he talked about what happened in Bardo, and it makes me wonder why the gods would break apart such a well-functioning team? They just promoted you, for gods' sake. They told you he's part of this thing happening with Lord Syrael, but I think it's bigger than that." I wind up my speech with a good gulp of wine.

"Then why didn't the mating bond activate when you had sex?" Tristan asks.

"She'll have a theory about that too," Troy says, with the note of pride and appreciation about the way my mind works.

Tristan feeds me another morsel from the tray. "Let's hear it."

"Cass is using magic that's blocking the brand. That has to be it, right? Because if this power you say came from me is strong enough to burn me and throw Cass across the room, why isn't he badly hurt? You said he was fine, and he sure looked fine. What went on after the bright light? What did you guys feel through your triplet connection."

Troy gives a you're-preaching-to-the-choir nod. Tristan looks thoughtful and feeds me a few more morsels while he's considering. I have to admit I'm loving having two guys who adore me and dote on me.

"I sensed your desire for Cass, which in itself is a clue," Troy says, "and suddenly you were screaming the word no, and fear and terror ripped through that place you now have in my heart. It's as if I've grown another heart, but it's yours."

"We could tell from our connection with Cass that something had gone wrong on his end. By the time we arrived, Cass was slumped against the wall, unconscious. Divine light surrounded you like a force field of some sort, and we couldn't get near you. I revived Cass while Troy tried to break through to you," Tristan says.

"What did he say when he came to?" I ask.

"He didn't say anything," Troy says. "He took off. "After a few minutes, your divine light dimmed, and you fainted, probably from the pain of your burns. Tristan used our combined magic to generate enough power to heal your wounds."

"The bastard's using magic to block us," Tristan says.

"He knows better. That's against the rules." Troy vaults into parental mode as if he's always been good about following rules. I smother an eye roll.

"He's not blocking you," I say. "He's protecting himself. That's what I'm trying to get you two to see."

"Let's say what you're telling us is true. There's not much we can do. We can't force love," Troy says as he massages the back of my neck, reminding me to release the tension.

"This isn't about us. We need to focus on Cass's fears," I say. "We need to show him we value him for more than his ability to take care of us. That we need him, need his love."

"Sounds like one of your fucking romance novels," Troy grumbles. "That's not how life works."

I throw some extra dumbass measure into the look I send him. "That's exactly how life works. Love and truth trump shame and fear. Always." I give a fist pump. "It's the law of nature. And if I can overcome my reaction to Cass's disdain, so can you. Really, Troy, it's about time you start believing in the power of love."

"I never said I don't believe in love. I love you, don't I?" Troy gives me his put-upon look.

Oh boy, just when things were going so well, I put my foot right up my ass.

"Babe, I'm not talking about you. In your words, why are you personalizing this? You have to admit your approach to sex is more clinical than emotional." Not my most empathic response.

"Would you two cut it out?" The command in Tristan's tone brings us both to attention. "Let's let the Cass dilemma percolate tonight and talk about it tomorrow."

"He's right. Cass will be a work in progress requiring more thought. We've got plans for tonight." Troy's switch in gears is swift and uncharacteristic, signaling that the "plans" will involve sex. "We've arranged an astronomy picnic for you." He points to my computer. "Get rid of that thing and change. Wear the clothes on the bed, nothing else."

A hot cylinder of desire ignites in my core at the familiar note of command in his voice.

Both guys start cleaning up the remnants of our snack, piling everything neatly on the tray.

"As thrilling as that sounds, I'm dying here, guys. What's the verdict on my article?" I ask cautiously.

"You know more about this writing stuff than I do," Troy says. "From my perspective, it's great, but I do have a couple of questions we'll discuss on the picnic."

"Like?" I ask.

"Like if I was that boring in the sex department," Troy says with a grin.

"I never—"

"Said I was boring, I know. We'll talk later." Troy's grin lets me know that whatever he has planned won't be what one would call boring.

"I echo Troy's sentiment," Tristan says. His smile is much naughtier than Troy's. "I want to hear more about this Nick guy you talk about in the diary."

Dear god. My ears are probably damned near purple, judging from the heat boiling through me. Troy and Tristan head off toward our villa. I follow, enjoying the warm sand on my feet while I decide which one has the best butt. I'm still not happy about the way things are with Cass. Hell, I'm not even sure I like the guy, and he certainly doesn't like me. His reaction to me is probably the main reason I'm getting so many migraines. I'm subconsciously internalizing his dislike. No matter how hard I try, emotional distress takes its toll on me physically.

But, now that Troy and Tristan have taken up residence in my heart, I have a certainty about life on steroids. The day I'd looked into Troy's eyes and known he meant it when he'd discovered his love was until death do us part had been one of the best in my life. Several hundred layers of insecurity had dropped off my shoulders, knowing I was no longer alone. His love at my back is what gave me the strength to face the world, and now I have Tristan's as well. I send a silent prayer to the heavens that Tristan's ability to heal sickness connected to Cass will give me the courage I need to lean into the discomfort of facing Cass. Time enough to figure all that out tomorrow. Tristan is right; I need the mental and physical break that only comes from sex with my guys.

When we reached the villa, I called dibs on the outdoor tub. Tristan and Troy each took one of the outdoor showers and were finished well before me. Troy paused on his way inside, and my eyes immediately fastened on the tent in the towel. The wicked grin I don't see enough of breaks and flickers of lust flash in his eyes. I so can't wait to explore this new stage of life with Troy. And now with Tristan.

"The outfit's on the bed. We'll meet you in the kitchen. Don't take all night." Troy bends to give me a swift kiss then disappears.

I luxuriate in the warm bath a few minutes longer, but I'm too impatient to see what my men have in store for me to linger. After toweling off and applying body lotion, I catch sight of a package that looks identical to the box holding the bottle of classic *L'air du Temps* perfume Troy had unearthed for me before he fell ill. *Ahhhh.* Love and tenderness flow through me at this reminder of just how far this man will go to please me. Except, he's not a man, he's an angel, and a whole new world of adventure lies ahead with him and his brothers. Smile firmly fixed on my face, I squirt the perfume in the air and walk through the mist toward the bedroom door. Scent should be subtle and something to explore, not something to announce my arrival. Two steps later, a band starts to tighten around my chest. My mind rapidly flips through a series of index cards. *That's weird. It can't be the endocrine because I've been faithful with my pills.*

Two more steps and I realize I'm having trouble breathing and that terrible buzzing pain is back. The perfume bottle falls out of my hand and crashes to the floor as my hand freezes. Oh shit. My body isn't the cause; magic is. **Troy!** I scream his name as loud as I can in my mind as blackness rises in front of me. I make it to the edge of the bed and slide to the floor. Strong arms lift me, but it's too dark for me to see whose.

"Did you give this to her?" Troy's voice is fading with the light.

"I thought you did." Tristan's voice is the last thing I hear before the mirror's eye opens and swallows my world.

"You are mine."

BLACK ROSE AND THE THREE PRINCES

THE FAIRY TALE CONTINUES . . .

Devastated, believing the archangel had killed Black Rose, the princes placed her in a glass coffin and took her soul to Bardo, the realm between lives. After hearing her story from the princes, Hera, Queen of the Gods, dislodged the piece of poisoned apple from Black Rose's throat, magically reviving her.

Syrael, who traced Black Rose through her ether, tried to snatch her from Hera's chambers. A battle of power ensued, during which Syrael mortally wounded the princes. Hera asked the Druids to hide Black Rose somewhere in the cosmos. The Druids cast a spell that cloaked Black Rose's identity and natural powers, a spell that could only be undone by Black Rose's willing consent to be taken by her one true love. As further protection, the Druids removed Black Rose's memories and placed her with a foster family on Earth, not knowing the foster father's true nature as a child abuser who would use his power to control and manipulate the child.

13

ALEAH

"You are mine." The eye in Lord Syrael's fucking magic mirror yawns open as life slips from me.

Adrenaline bolts through my system as my airway closes and the mirror's eye widens and moves forward to consume me. I'm not frightened so much as determined—I'd rather die before I let another man control me, and if this is death, it's not so bad. I could live without the between stage as pain grips me, and I fight a losing battle for air.

Then, something shoves me. Hard. And, in nine-tenths of a second, I'm back in the sensory deprivation chamber that reminds me of The Nothing in *The Neverending Story* where I dropped the first time Syrael attacked me. Thankfully, the pain stops as I lose all sensation from my corporeal being. It takes me another thirteen seconds to add two plus two. If I'm right, my Brad Pitt fantasy in the form of Joe Black should appear any time. For a split second, his name eludes me. *Fuck*. Ever since I hit early menopause, my memory for names has all but disappeared. It's something familiar. *Steve. John.*

Sure enough, the warmth and light that signal his appearance seeps into the void around me. The threads connecting me to Troy and Tristan stretch thin. I grab one in each hand and hold it tight. As long as I have Troy's love, everything will work out. Tristan's love makes that a certainty. But, back to—*Bob.*

"Bob. Still running from your destiny, I see." Bob raises his left eyebrow and extends his wings just like he did the first time we met. He assumes the same position, leaning against something invisible and crossing his legs at the ankles. He's wearing a black leather jacket, a gray button-down shirt and black jeans on this visit. I do have to admit that a little something tickles my lady bits as I take in that gorgeous smile. I eye him up and down with an appraising eye. I mean after all, if I'm going to embrace this idea of having multiple husbands, I might as well go all in.

The bastard winks at me. "Trust me when I tell you I'm not part of your destiny." His grin is almost as charming as Tristan's. "We have our hands full with Tate."

I cross my not-quite-corporeal arms over my chest and heave a mighty dramatic sigh. "So, let me guess. You're here to tell me it's not my time yet and to let me know more about why your Tate thinks my brain isn't engaged."

For a split second, I consider whether dumping a load of snark on the Angel of Death is a good idea and give a mental shrug. What's the worst he can do? Send me to Bardo? That might not be a bad idea. From what I've gathered, they have a hell of a lot more sex than I'm getting. I'm *totally* pouting about missing my first threesome.

I give him my most charming smile and send a silent prayer to the gods to give me just one of those flirty girlie genes so I can charm the ass off this angel. If I'm ever given three wishes, one of them will be to channel Mae West, but back to reality.

"I'm ready." I'm talking about being sent back to my

picnic, but I give a mental fist pump at my double entendre. Maybe there's something to this Mae West stuff.

My reward for the snark is another charming grin. "That's the spirit, and I'm happy to hear you're ready." Bob winks at me again. "I see you took our advice and got laid. Good work. Even better, you're getting past that shame you carry around like a prize." Bob retracts his wings and starts pacing in front of me. "But I'm here to see if we're mistaken in our assessment of you."

That gets my attention, and I armor up. If there's one thing I know, it's what criticism looks like. "Meaning?"

"Meaning we may have been mistaken in our belief that you're a Nephilim, one of the chosen. If we're wrong about you, we'll be having a very different discussion."

It doesn't take a rocket scientist to know that my life with Troy might be in danger, and I'm fighting for all I hold dear. People in positions of power and privilege have been trying to control me my entire life, and this Angel of Death is no exception. I may be new to all this magic stuff, but one thing is for sure in any universe, if I'm not one of the chosen, I'm mortal and will have my ass bounced back to my regular life.

I try not to fidget under the heat of Bob's appraising gaze as the thoughts tumble through my head. I take a deep cleansing breath and reach past the emotions rushing through me. A thought hits me, and I narrow my gaze at him.

"Negative psychology doesn't work well on me. You're better off telling me what you have to say. We both know that I'm more than a mere mortal." My shoulders straighten as pride flows through me. "I have the power of divine light." I have no idea if that's the correct terminology to use with all this magic stuff, but he'll get the gist.

"You're making this sound like some job interview when it isn't. I either am one of the chosen, or I'm not. And if you all would give me a goddamn minute, I might be able to figure it all out." I finish in a huff. It's probably not the smartest thing to try to shame an angel.

"I apologize for snapping at you." I give Bob an apologetic smile as I come back into my right mind. "What are your concerns?"

"It occurred to us that you might have some questions about what all this means. There's a lot we can't explain. The prophecy says there's much you need to discover on your own; however, I can tell you about the nature of the position you'll hold." Bob resumes his lounging position against the invisible counter.

The news about a position perks me right up, and visions of a large office nestled somewhere on a celestial cloud spring to mind. Sadly, the reality is usually nowhere near my fantasies. I need more information before I get too excited, but my damned heart does a fast cha-cha at the prospect of a job involving wielding superpowers.

"The gods need someone to coordinate the efforts of the sex angel lords. Someone to help them prioritize their work, find appropriate missions and fight on the front lines. They think that person is you." Bob gives me a panty-melting smile that rivals Tristan's and takes the edge off his tone. "In addition to your strong values and untainted sexual soul, we need your natural leadership strengths. The sex angel lords need your unconditional love and strength to help them overcome their challenges. The prophecy says that your divine bond will allow the four of you to combine your power, making it more than enough to defeat Syrael and his minions."

"Two questions. How many of these sex angel lords am I mating with, and what do you expect me to do?"

"Three and take your place as their divine mate. You want the straight goods, so I'll give them to you. You are Nephilim. This *is* your destiny. The rest will come naturally to you."

Bob isn't subtle about the emphasis on the word "is." So much for it being my decision.

"So, if I understand you correctly, you want me to get on board with this calling of yours and speed up the process of helping Cass see the light."

"That about covers it. We want you to slay your doubt dragons and get on with the job." The Angel of Death drops me a wink making it clear he's not threatening, simply making a statement of fact. "You've been training for this calling since you were born. It's time to take the reins. What do you need to make that happen? If it's within my power to give, it's yours."

"A safe place where we can rest and work on finding my powers. A base to work from." Hope springs eternal that discovering my power will call for a lot more sex, but we don't need to get specific. I push up my glasses and smooth my curls behind my ears taking an extra split second of thought. "Of course, it would make things a lot simpler if you gods just give me my powers now."

Bob gives me a smile that's damned near parental with pride. "I know just the place, and no can do. You must find your own magic. Those are the rules. But it's been my experience that the blessed know their gifts on an intuitive level. Follow your gut." He reaches into his jacket pocket and pulls out a square the size of a money clip that looks like wood.

Ornately engraved scroll work runs along the top and bottom of a carved wooden tablet. On corresponding sides of the tablet lie carvings of a naked woman and three men, shown with intricate detail. And they're having an orgy. Inscribed on one side are the words "Ticket to Temptation" and on the other "The Chosen One."

I bite my bottom lip hard to keep from moaning. Something in that piece of wood calls to me like some magical aphrodisiac. Bob smiles again. The guy sure is happy, considering the nature of his job.

"The Druids have offered you a safe haven for as long as you wish. This ticket grants access to their lands. You can't take this through the void, so it will be waiting for you when you revive. The gods protect the Manor, so you'll be safe from Syrael's magic mirror."

He winks one last time, ejects his wings, and disappears. Intense burning pain lets me know I'm back on Earth and a long way from my frigging picnic.

14

TRISTAN

Severe pain searing through me is the only warning I have that Aleah's coming back to us. The instant we realized dark magic infused the perfume, we'd stripped Aleah and submerged her in the freshwater plunge pool. The special connection we share has dimmed, but it's still there giving my pounding heart a measure of hope. *Come back to us,* mon chou.

A flash of bright light almost blinds me, and my eyelids snap shut against the assault. Several seconds later, they spring open at the sound of a somewhat familiar voice.

"Greetings, gentlemen." Bob, the Angel of Death, stands at the side of the large outdoor saltwater pool where Troy and I frantically try to wash away the remnants of the poison perfume from Aleah's inert form.

"Aleah asked for a safe place where you three can gather your wits and come up with a new game plan. I'm here to deliver the ticket you'll need to gain access to Blackstone Manor. As long as you're on the manor grounds, you're protected from all supernatural power and magic except your own. That will allow you to help the Chosen take control of her power." Bob takes a few steps and places something on the wicker sofa facing the pool. He straightens and throws a bemused look our way as if letting us know he can relate to our situation. "Now, if you gentlemen will excuse me."

"Where's Aleah?" Troy's hard voice hides the fear we're both trying not to acknowledge. As the words leave his mouth, Ali moans and her limbs start to shake.

"She's right behind me," Bob says casually, exploring the exotic outdoor bathroom as if he's never seen one before. "This attack was more powerful than the last, but she'll be good as new with a good night's rest and a couple of injections of divine essence. Blackstone Manor will give her the chance to recover and regroup."

Troy and I exchange relieved glances as we send a silent prayer of thanks to the gods.

"Thank you for bringing her back to us," Troy says. "It seems I'm in your debt yet again."

Ali groans.

Bob hunkers down at the edge of the pool. "No thanks needed." Bob examines Ali as she starts to shiver. "The gods are more convinced than ever that your Aleah is the chosen one proclaimed in the prophecy. The magic of Blackstone Manor will accelerate the development of her powers. She's coming around, so I'll be off and leave you to it."

"Hold on just a godsdamned minute," Cass demands. He stands from where he's crouched by the side of the pool and strides over to Bob. He snatches the ticket from Bob's hand and points it at his chest. "What makes this place so much safer than our sanctuary here?"

Being the angel of death, he's unperturbed by Cass's aggressive advance. He raises an eyebrow and stands his ground. "Blackstone Manor sits in the middle of an ancient Druid ceremonial ground that's been protected by the combined power of the Olympian and Druid gods for thousands of years. The grounds are only visible to those who hold a Ticket to Temptation."

"She's going home tomorrow, so we won't be needing your ticket," Cass says.

"Shut the fuck up, Cassiel." My use of his full name shows him just how pissed off at his behavior I am. "We'll do what we need to keep her safe."

Aleah makes a loud moan and starts to thrash in our arms.

"I'll take that as my cue to leave. The caretaker, Raphael, will be there when you arrive at the manor. He can answer all your questions." Bob makes a slight gesture with his hand and opens a portal. He glances at Ali then without another word steps through and disappears leaving a soft chuckle in his wake.

"Oh, God." Aleah curls into the fetal position and starts panting.

Slow, measured thoughts flow through me as she works through the pain from Syrael's poison coursing around in her system. *Breathe. Breathe. You can do this. Embrace the pain. In, two, three, four, hold, two, three, four, out, two, three, four, hold, two, three, four.*

Troy sweeps Aleah from my arms into his and lowers her dripping form to the nearby wicker sofa. He crouches beside her and looks up at me. "Can't you do anything for her?" Raw pain from post-magic hypothermia tears through our connection to her, and Troy fights his need to flee and lick his emotional wounds. As angelic princes born triplets to archangels, Cass, Troy, and I are blessed—or cursed depending on whose point of view you're taking—with a telepathic connection. Triplets are divinity in the Old Religion and gifted with exceptional power that we could share through our connection. Troy's fighting the urge to flee for self-preservation. I beam a firm grip of support through our telepathic connection.

"My healing powers only work on Syrael's dark magic when combined with my ether." I look down at Ali as uncontrollable shivering seizes her. "What seems to work the best is when we have a three-way connection. Our combined grace should help ease the symptoms."

"We can't do this now. We're not safe here. We've got to go," Cass says.

Troy ignores him and sits, pulling Ali's head into his lap. I sit beside him, one hand on her bare leg with the other on Troy's shoulder. As soon as the connection is made, strands of blue grace rise from each of us. Blue-white, sapphire, and teal blue strands twist together to form a rope glittering with our divine essence.

I watch with wonder as the rope weaves around the three of us in an intricate pattern and her energy latches onto our grace and absorbs it. Slowly, her moans diminish, and her body relaxes.

Ali loops an arm around Troy's neck without opening her eyes, pulls herself up, and rests her head against his chest. She grabs my neck and pulls my head to her chest, opening our connection even more. We sit bound together as our heartbeats slow and synchronize. Eventually, Cass's manic pacing makes him impossible to ignore. Ali tightens her grip on my neck, opening a flow of love and strength that damned near knocks me over. Troy leans his head back and sighs as her love washes away his distress. We stay this way, suspended, for several long, glorious moments before she pushes off Troy's chest. She's not strong enough to hold herself up but tries to cover the weakness as she collapses back against Troy's chest.

"Cass is right. We've got to go before the mirror finds me again. I can still feel it. We'd better go now." Ali looks at me as if she knows I'm about to go mad without something to focus on and gives me a small smile. "Do you mind bringing my stuff?" She lists off the "stuff" in her mind as Troy picks her up and heads toward the portal Cass opens. Using my rusty telekinetic power, I gather the items on Ali's list and follow the others into the portal.

We step out onto a tree-shrouded road that suddenly opens up to a sunlit expanse of manicured lawn, a large open circle cut out in the middle of the forest. Except for the lane, trees surround the oasis, similar to the walls of a castle. At the back of the clearing stands a beautiful old two-story house with fieldstone walls, gables and white pillars forming a wraparound porch. Warm light reflects off huge windows flanked with shutters. The narrow lane continues around the house and looks like the only access point.

As we draw closer, the house reveals unique qualities usually attributed to tradespeople's lost skills from the turn of the twentieth century. Our surroundings are stunning to the point that it seems unreal. As if a magical place has been hidden away in the middle of a forest in small-town America. I pause and listen to the stillness, inhaling the scents of dew-damp foliage, rich soil, and sweet flowers. As much as I love the tropics, the forest is where nature speaks to me. I tip my face to the sun breaking through the foliage and let serenity wash over me. I'll be able to find my stillness here.

The place is well maintained, immaculate even. Four inlaid stone steps lead up to a double front door with opaque beveled glass that looks like lead crystal. Wicker chairs are scattered invitingly along the wraparound porch.

Unlike the sensation of calm the grounds give me, something about the house supercharges me, fills me with static electricity, like an impending storm, ready to burst forth at any second. I haven't felt this alive since cliff diving from Mount Olympus.

Cass marches up to the door and grasps the knocker—a solid brass plate with a hinged ring overlay. Upon closer inspection, the right half of the ring is a life-sized phallus, curving down to meet the pouting lips of an inviting labia. Unusual, to say the least, definitely very odd. Elaborate scrollwork etched into the door above the knocker reads, *Please knock.* Cass does, and the heavy door glides open. An elderly gentleman, resplendent in a beautifully tailored suit, stands silently before us. His navy suit is cut in a style from some bygone era; my guess is the early nineteen-thirties based on the elevated waistline and the wide peaked corners of the lapels.

His age is an enigma; I can only guess at it. His gray hair and the lines on his face conflict with the erect posture indicating a hidden strength generally found in younger men. A warm smile gives the impression he's meeting old friends he hadn't seen in years. His voice reinforces the sentiment.

"Welcome to my home. I'm so pleased you found your way, Cassiel." The man has a definite spark of mischief in his eyes.

"Do I know you?" Cass steps back as sparkling dark-chocolate brown eyes take in our bedraggled sopping wet appearance.

"Where are my manners? I hope you can forgive an old man for his less-than-acceptable manners with such a charming visitor to his home." His gaze glances over Troy and me but holds on to Ali. A small, thoughtful smile stretches his lips before he gives his head a shake.

"Let me introduce myself. My name is Raphael, and it is a pleasure to make your acquaintance." He raises his hand, and our clothes dry instantly.

Raphael holds his hands out, palms open, and bows, ever so slightly, in what reminds me of an act of contrition before he steps aside. With another slight bow, he sweeps his arm in a wide arc gesturing for us to go in. Troy steps forward with Ali, who rests in his arms, eyes closed.

We step into a dimly lit hall. Sconces and what looked like original oil paintings lined the walls. I catch a glimpse of several nudes of a beautiful woman.

"Which way to our room?" Troy asks.

Raphael points ahead to a large wooden staircase polished to a golden shine. Each carved spindle represents a wooden phallus. "You'll find the master bedroom on your right at the far end of the hall."

Troy heads up the stairs while Cass marches after Raphael. I hesitate for a moment, then follow Cass. Right now, Ali needs sleep, and Troy doesn't need my help settling her into bed.

Raphael leads the way down the hall and into what looks like a vast living room. I can't help but gape as I look around the distinctive architecture. Wood and stone sculptures, large and small, adorn every nook and cranny in the room. All depict one or more people in the throes of sexual congress. Some display exaggerated anatomy, teasing the imagination of the observer. Raphael leads us into the next room, a retro kitchen, and from there into a study lined from floor to ceiling with bookcases. The room instantly becomes my new happy place. The gods couldn't have chosen a more perfect sanctuary for the three of us to explore our new bond. Fuck Cass if he chooses not to join us.

Raphael sits in an armchair and gestures toward the sofa and chairs that form a square around a large low table strewn with books and a china tea service on a tray. "Perhaps you would be kind enough to join me for some tea?"

Cass glowers, and I step forward before he cuts this gracious old man off.

"Manners, Cassiel."

"We'd love to, thank you," I say.

Cass gives a curt nod and sits beside me on the very edge of the thickly upholstered leather couch.

"Wonderful." Raphael slides the tray toward him and lifts the teapot. "There's nothing quite as soothing as hot tea made with spring water and just a hint of lemon and honey."

I relax and take a good look around as Raphael expertly dresses our tea. This house, like the man before us, whispers of a bygone era. I look up at the fifteen-foot ceiling and handcrafted shelves loaded with books. Its splendor and understated elegance draw me in, and I take a moment to inhale the ambiance. When I shut my eyes, I'm almost sure I catch a whiff of a fine cigar permeating the weirdly intoxicating smell of paper, ink, and leather.

Raphael sits back in his leather chair and raises his china cup. "Please, join me."

I reach over to pick up my cup and saucer and freeze, staring at the tray. I shut my eyes tight, sure I'm hallucinating. Had the woman painted on the tray just winked at me? I've seen a lot of things, but this is a new one. I open my eyes, and sure enough, there she is sketched in perfect graphic and very explicit detail—a naked woman, groping herself, her head thrown back in the throes of orgasm. Looking directly at me. She doesn't find sex humiliating, degrading, or just plain dull. For this woman, sex is pure pleasure and joy.

I looked up to find Raphael's calm eyes studying me as if measuring my response. "It's quite remarkable. I hope I didn't shock you."

No, of course not. I'm a sex angel lord, after all, and it's every day someone serves me a side of naked woman along with my tea.

"No, no. Just unexpected," I say. "It's so lifelike, and what a beautiful woman. It's quite surreal."

Surreal, now that was an understatement. Everything about this place screams magic, yet something made it all seem so peaceful, so natural.

"Oh, she's quite real, and Lady B's beauty was legendary. Her name was Anais Blackstone. She is the reason this house exists. It's her sanctuary to spiritual enlightenment and immortality."

Cass gets up abruptly and strolls around the room. "Is this Anais the entity I sense?"

"She is, and you're blessed indeed if she's chosen to welcome you personally. Very blessed indeed." Raphael takes another sip of his tea.

I join him, trying to calm the excitement and anticipation coursing through me. Our entity, as Cass calls her, is a ghost. Her visage is vague and misty, but this older version of the woman on the tray claps her hands in delight. Something about this house makes one thing clear in a way it hadn't been before. Our lives are about to change, and there's no going back now.

15

ALEAH

Awareness slowly brushes away the cobwebs left from crazy dreams and the aftereffects of my latest trip into the void. Two warm, naked bodies flank me, and a soft snore punctuates the early morning silence. The scent of eroticism washes over me, and for an instant, I'm sure it's coming from the very pores of the old house. It's penetrating. Insistent. Just like my guys had been last night. I snuggle deeper and let the muscle memory of my assault on them last night wash over me. I'd taken what I needed from both men without regard for their satisfaction. A blush of embarrassment tries to surface and is kicked firmly in the ass by my new alter ego. Much of what happened after Bob brought me back is vague right up until the moment I'd awakened, but I remember every detail of my attack on Troy and Tristan.

When we entered our room, Troy's concerned gaze had lit a fuse of lust that exploded through my hands as I pushed him onto his back and knelt over his cock. "Don't talk," I hissed before I swallowed his hard cock in one swift movement of my warm, wet mouth. My connection to each of the guys changed to a flowing current. I used current to channel my need for their healing essence. Spreading my knees wide, I mentally commanded Tristan to fuck me. Hard.

Nothing existed but raw instinct and feeding my need with these two men because consuming their very essence would make me whole. Each time one of them tried to slow my frenetic pace, I used the strength of my mind to subdue them, to bend them to my will. I set a frantic pace and lost myself to fucking and being fucked. Moans of agonized ecstasy tore through us as their explosive orgasms forced their essence into me. And at that moment, something within me broke free. Something I knew I'd figure out in the morning as I drifted back to sleep. It had all been so instinctual as if I were dreaming. If I was, it was the best fucking dream of my life. Pun intended.

I barely move a muscle, but it's enough for Troy to tighten his grasp on my butt cheek. Troy sighs and tucks the hand he's holding under his chin. Smiling, I slowly open my eyes and stare up at a painting of a stunning woman lying on a chaise lounge. Draped with some gauzy material that's intertwined around her limbs, she's reaching out to two incredibly handsome young men relaxing at either end of the lounge, gazing at her with adoration. I could swear she's looking down on us with approval.

Heat sweeps through me, igniting the smoldering flame that's been lit, and for the first time since Troy got sick, I'm pumped to meet the day. I harken back to my management days when I'd met my new team. It's a new day, and I'm armed and ready to meet it. Angel Bob kicked my make-things-happen strength in the butt, and Activator strength answered the call. Time to retake charge of my life.

The extraordinary places in my heart that appeared with each mating bond assure me that Troy and Tristan are with me for the dance no matter how it ends. And now that I know Cass is coming from a place of hurt and shame that's very clear when I look at him objectively. I understand the burden of accepting the role of caregiver at an early age and the baggage that goes along with it. I'd filled the role of "mom" for my foster parents' four children. Hell, they still call me for advice even though we're well into our middle years. For a long time, I'd believed that family was about obligation, not love, so I recognize the signs in Cass now that I'm looking for them. And now, there's a small voice deep inside that's getting stronger, telling me I'm just the woman to bring him into the fold.

Troy's hand slides between my legs and pauses, a silent inquiry. Spontaneity is a rare event for Troy, possibly nonexistent, even with sex. He won't proceed without giving me the chance to object. Tristan has no such reservations, and his hand slides over my breast as he makes his silent appeal.

"Oh, no you don't." I push up and throw the covers off. "I've got things to do, and I need your help."

Two strong arms pull me back onto the bed, and Troy draws the covers up before the two of them wrestle me back into a compliant position.

"If you two don't let me up, I'm going to pee all over you. My bladder is that full," I announce cheerfully. Two hot bodies roll onto their backs with groans and arms thrown over their eyes.

The smell of delicious baked goods drifts on the air. "Dibs on the bathroom. I'll meet you in the kitchen in fifteen minutes." I hop off the bed and scoot into the bathroom, closing the door firmly behind me.

The eyes in the mirror are alive with energy and anticipation. I stare at the face looking back at me, searching for hints to my powers. I open my eyes wide a few times and try snapping my fingers, something I'd never done well in the first place. I spend moments contorting my face while I try to wish my magic powers into existence. Nothing but a massive hot flash hits me. No hint of magic, but plenty of reminders that I'm menopausal.

I flip through my memory banks for what I know about magic and superpowers. As a kid, I'd gone through a stage when I'd been obsessed with the supernatural. When I'd found reruns of the TV show *Bewitched*, I'd watched every single episode at least twice. Like Samantha, I try wiggling my nose and look something like a cow chewing cud. Nothing power-wise and not cute while I'm at it. With a sigh, I splash cold water on my face to break the heat and head into the shower.

After my shower, I don the bathrobe hanging on the back of the door and shiver. Time to find something to wear. I open a sliding door and step into a magnificent room stuffed with elegant dresses, gowns, and every manner of fancy lingerie I could think of. None of it looked inexpensive. All of it looked as if it hailed from the early 1930s. I get lost for a few minutes exploring the massive wardrobe, indulging my love of clothes.

I choose a white knit short-sleeved sweater and navy-blue twill culottes with a high fitted waist and slip them on over a silk chemise and bloomers. They fit as if they're tailored for me. I give a nod of appreciation to the previous owner while I pull on a pair of embroidered black kid-leather pumps with a Louis heel.

"You're most welcome, my child. I'm glad you like them." A low melodic voice sounds behind me, and I damned near swallow my tongue with fright. A ghostly apparition, drifts into my line of sight. A misty older version of the woman in the painting from the ceiling of my bedroom smiles down at me.

"Welcome to Blackstone Manor. We've been waiting for you,"

"Who are you?" My three-and-a-half octave vocal range squeaks into the upper ranges.

"My name is Anais Blackstone, but you may call me Nye. That's what my great-great-grandson calls me, and the look on your face reminds me of the first time he was here. Or you can call me Lady B if that turns your crank."

One thousand and sixty-nine questions bubble in my brain, but I'm suddenly struck with the wisdom of middle age and manage to keep my mouth shut. I plaster an enquiring look on my face and fold my hands in my lap.

"We have plenty of time to answer your questions. You're under the Druid gods' protective power, and this sanctuary is contained within our sacred ceremonial grounds. Lord Syrael cannot reach you here. As the high priestess, I'm here to guide you as you find your power and learn how to use it. Raphael is keeper of the house's magic, and he'll see to your needs." She gives me a sly little grin. "I hear you need a few lessons in the erotic arts. Fascinating that one who loves sex so much can know so little about her inner desires. Now, you'd better get moving. You're the lady of the manor, and the manor's magic is at your disposal. Oh, and by the way, your lion's about to burst from his cage." And she disappears, but I know exactly who she's referring to. Cass is about to have a conniption.

I run a comb through my curls while my head brims with ideas and discoveries. I've seen a ghost, and this Blackstone Manor wraps around me like a warm hug. As the smiling face in the mirror looks back at me and gives a high five, I realize I'm not wearing my glasses, and I can see perfectly. *Fucking, eh!* Feeling every bit of the kick-ass forty-year-old lady of the manor, I follow the smells to the kitchen.

Just as Nye predicted, Cass looks as if he's about to crawl out of his skin, and before I do anything else, I need to clear the air.

"Morning, boys," I say as I pass Troy and Tristan and come to a stop a couple of feet from Cass. He glares down at me. I glare right back, praying I don't get a crick in my neck while refusing to look away first. I'm on a mission, and no frigging guy with muscles is going to deter me.

"I apologize if I got a little heated yesterday. You're right. I came barging in here like a bull in a china shop. I know you're doing what's best for you and your brothers. I'll try to work within that. Can we start over?"

Cass studies me as if trying to figure out what I'm up to, but his guard is down, so I press my advantage while I have the element of surprise. I reach up and place my palm on the side of his face. The jolt of electricity confirms Troy's suspicion that Cass in also my destined mate. Cass stumbles back as if he's been hit with a hot brand and claps a hand to his cheek.

I give him my best so-sorry smile. "Static electricity. Sorry. It won't happen again."

Cass drops his hand, sends a wary smile in my direction and mutters something that sounds like, "No problem. It happens."

Knowing that Cass is one of my destined mates changes my perspective. It's as clear as the sweet fall air coming in through the open windows. Troy had given me lots of practice dealing with the male gender's morbid fear of the ball and chain. I turn so I can hide the satisfaction coursing through me and run smack into the chest of a tall, thin older man with impeccable bearing, every bit like an aristocratic butler. This must be the caretaker Nye talked about.

"Domina Aleah. Welcome to the manor." Mr. Courtly gathers my right hand in his, bows and kisses the back of it. "Raphael, at your service, Domina."

I gape at the strange man in horror. What conceivable thing would give him the idea I'm a dominatrix. Strong and capable is one thing, but I have no desire to don vinyl—I have enough problems with hot flashes—and get all bossy pants on a man. That would require entirely more thought and physical exertion than I'm willing to expend to get laid. No siree, I'm not the cabana boy type. No, my cavemen would grab me by the hair and drag me off to bed as long as they have no problem with me joining the hunt as an equal partner the next day. I snatch my hand out of Raphael's and take a step back. "You must have mistaken me for someone else. I'm not a dominatrix."

"No, Domina," Raphael says gravely, "you are not. The furthest thing from it, actually. I use the honorific to confer rank or, in your case, acknowledge you hold a barony. High Priestess Anais has assigned you all the rights and privileges and magic of Blackstone Manor, Domina." He bows again and steps back.

I gape at him for several long seconds while I process this new development and, thirteen seconds later, decide fuck it. Time to roll with the punches.

16

ATROYEL

I throw on a pair of jeans, a T-shirt, and a hoodie against the chill of the autumn air and head out to find coffee. Bright white walls and white cupboards flanking stained glass windows greet me as I enter the kitchen and check out the fridge. In addition to the staples, the well-stocked fridge, circa 1920, holds everything from cold cuts and an impressive selection of cheeses to complete meals. Either the caretaker loves to cook, or he's a most thoughtful host, maybe both. One thing for sure; we won't need to worry about food during our stay. After giving a nod to Cass and Tristan, I help myself to a coffee and lean against the counter in the large airy kitchen letting my thoughts drift to their favorite place.

I could tell from the moment that Aleah's eyes popped open this morning that something fundamental had changed for her. But, if I'd had any doubt, the set of her shoulders and determined footsteps as she enters the kitchen removed it. My beauty has her spunk back and then some. She marches past Tristan and me with an I'll-get-to-you-later wave.

When she stops in front of Cass, I wonder for a split second if she's going to slap him, but instead, she places her palm on the side of his face. Cass reacts as if the touch is a blow and stumbles backward. I exchange a surprised glance with Tristan. He shrugs back.

We all feel the sizzle of electricity as it hits Cass. The computer that hums at the back of Aleah's brain is back to operating at full capacity. Cass looks stunned. This time, Tristan and I exchange a grin. We know just how the poor bastard feels when hit with that first connection with Aleah. He's felt the first prick of the hook and will flop around trying to swim free. But and before he knows it, he'll have bitten down on the barb, and she'll reel him in.

The caretaker materializes out of nowhere and introduces himself to Aleah. He assures her he's here to meet our every need and ushers us to the round table where Cass now sits, lost in thought.

"Tea with honey and lemon, Domina?" Raphael asks.

"Perfect, thank you." Aleah puts a notebook, phone, glasses, and pen in front of her plate. Raphael delivers a steaming cup of tea and refreshes our coffee. "Thank you again."

"Why aren't you wearing your glasses?" I ask. Not only is Aleah close to blind without her glasses, but they're also her shield against the unspoken advantages of white privilege she faced on Earth.

She puts her hand to her temple as if they're there and gives me that smile, the one that has always torn through the clouds of daily life and showered me with sunshine. "I can see without them. Awesome, right? I'm feeling better than I've felt in years. I'm afraid to even think about it in case I jinx it." She squeezes my thigh. Placing a hand on the back of her neck, I bring her face to mine and brush her lips. "You won't jinx anything, beauty. That's the magic working."

Somewhere along the line, I stopped being that selfish guy who would insist on her full attention and make her feel guilty to cover up my own insecurity. I want to show her she's taught me to be a better man. But even more, I want to know about what's going on in her head. But I know the best way to find out, and I can bide my time. I stamp down my usual impatience to get on with this next chapter of our lives.

"If you guys don't mind, I'd like to clear the air before we go about our day." She takes a few sips of tea while she waits for our nods. I can't help but smile as we help ourselves to the food Raphael quietly brings to the table. My beauty is back. I can relax and go along for the ride, my favorite place to be.

"Go ahead, babe, we're listening," Tristan says.

"I know I said I'd be leaving after the event tonight, but I was coming from a place of emotion, not intellect. Nye says we're protected here so we can relax and figure out what's going on."

"By Nye, may we presume you're speaking of Miss Blackstone?" Raphael purses his lips and narrows his eyes.

Aleah nods. "Yes, the high priestess. I think she's my designated spirit guide, so I'll be staying put."

"Who the fuck is Nye?" Cass asks. "Is someone else going to crawl out of the woodwork?"

Aleah tilts her head as if listening and looks in the direction of the wall above her head. We follow her gaze as that vague feeling we're not alone hits me again. After a moment, she grins and says, "I'll have to take your word for that."

"Who the fuck are you talking to?" Cass is more than a little irritated. He hates when things are outside of his control.

"I'm talking to the woman who owns this place, Anais Blackstone." Aleah works hard to keep the irritation out of her voice. She hates repeating herself, something she and Cass have in common. Cass's lousy mood is rubbing her the wrong way despite her best intentions. Aggressive men are a trigger for her, and our bond shows me the battle she's waging with her instinct to lash out. If he keeps this up, he won't know what hit him.

"She says you're a bit of a feisty one, and I'm going to have fun taming you. The alphas always fall the hardest, she says." Aleah's smile is pure evil, and I realize she's not put out. She's baiting him.

"You can see her." Raphael sounds almost reverent. He bows again as if he's visiting royalty.

Fucking, eh. Aleah's thought hits my brain loud and clear, but she looks at each of us and asks, "Am I the only one who can see her?"

"If I may, Domina," Raphael interjects with another bow, "it's remarkable *you* can see the high priestess. You are the first in over one hundred years she's revealed herself to. Not even her great-grandson can see her. You are one of the chosen." This time his head damned near reaches the floor when he bows.

"Why does he keep bowing?" I hiss in a stage whisper.

"I don't know, but go with it." Aleah answers in a matching stage whisper. "He's odd and magical and maybe even a time traveler. I think it's cultural."

When he straightens, he looks as if he's listening to the wall. "Yes, I stand corrected. Daniel is Miss Blackstone's great-great-grandson."

That pronouncement seems to be everyone's cue to collect their thoughts. Aleah's analytical side is on overdrive, and she's trying hard to ignore her delight in the new developments. We'll have to show her that she deserves all this and more.

I finish my plate of scrambled eggs and spread marmalade over a slice of toast. Raphael refreshes my coffee, complete with fresh cream reminding me of the service provided at the fine inns of New England Aleah loves visiting. I could get used to this lifestyle.

Tristan is the first to break the silence. "So, what's next, babe? Whatever you need, I'm game. Just tell me what to do."

Cass frowns. I wait. If Aleah wants something, she'll let me know. Otherwise, I'm free to enjoy the ride. And to do that, I need time alone to process where I'm at with the changes to our dynamic and relationship. Right now, we're in what Aleah calls the honeymoon phase. I'm so fucking happy to be reunited with her, I'll say yes to damned near anything. But Aleah gives Tristan a shy smile, reminding me that all of this is new to her.

"Bob says I have to discover my superpowers or magic or whatever I've got myself. Both he and Nye suggest that I've already been preparing for this day, and the only thing I've delved into is finding out who I am, what makes me tick. It's as if when I need to know something that will help me, an opportunity appears," Aleah says. "A few weeks ago, I felt compelled to start a book study about vulnerability and shame, and I can't shake the feeling that I'm learning something vital if I do the work."

"If I may, Domina—"

"If we want your opinion, old man, we'll ask for it," Cass says.

Aleah's gaze is laser-sharp as she focuses on him. "I have an ask of all of us. I'm working very hard to change old habits of naming and shaming to empathy and compassion. I know too well that intensely painful experience of having people point out that I'm flawed and unworthy of love or belonging. So I'll be calling it out when I see it, and I'll ask you to do the same. Empathy may come naturally to some sex angels, but you need to work on yours."

"You have a lot of work to do if you can't explain it without shaming me," Cass retorts.

They face off for several tense beats, and I wait for Aleah to deliver the knockout blow. She surprises me again when she says, "You're right. Inferring you aren't empathic is shaming. I apologize and thank you."

"For what, him being an asshole?" Tristan asks. Aleah pulls her lips in to hide her smile. I'm mesmerized as I watch this strong, confident woman who saved my sorry ass in more ways than she knows.

"If I may, Domina," Raphael tries again. With a quick suppressing look at Cass, Aleah smiles up at him.

"We are not permitted to help you find your powers, but we can let you know when you're taking the correct course. You will not go wrong by studying empathy. Or healing." He adds the last as if an afterthought as he walks away.

Tristan, never one to pass up an opportunity, gulps the last of his food and leans forward eagerly. "I could use a refresher course myself. How about I go with you, Ali? I found a great place where we can work."

"You might be sorry. Troy hates it when I go all psycho-babble on him." She grins at me and places a hand on mine. "Babe?"

"What a bunch of horse shit." Cass stalks out of the room. Tristan and I exchange a final glance. Aleah has her work cut out for her with this brother.

"You go ahead. I'll meet up with you later. Cass and I are going to check out this Acquired Taste club where the event is being held tonight. After last night's scare, I want to be double sure we know what we're stepping into." I grab her face and give her a quick but sound kiss. Anything more, and I'll rip her pants off and fuck her right here. She gives a small sigh and pushes back from the table.

"Come on, let's go." Tristan grabs Aleah's hand. She looks back at me as if reassuring herself that I'm okay. I hold her gaze for several long beats. I'm not at all surprised that she's destined for something great. Her strengths and gifts have always been evident to me. I'm grateful she seems to want me along for the ride. Only the blessed received the gift of Aleah's love. I have no idea why she chose me, but she did, and I'm never letting her go.

"Go have fun. I have plans for us later."

She smiles as the thought hits her mind. *"Promises, promises."* Her message plants itself in me as Tristan leads her away.

Oh beauty, I have a very special night planned for you.

17

ALEAH

Tristan proves to be a handy guy to have around, and I'm superficial enough to love being waited on. He arranges for Raphael to bring lunch and refreshments and, still clutching my hand, leads me into a place I instantly know will be home while I'm here, a combination library, office, and den. Another portrait of Anais hangs over the fireplace, and I could swear she's looking at me as I go to the desk. It should be creepy but its comforting, as if she's looking out for me. Her warm and comforting essence is tangible in the room.

I'd love to explore, but I'm fixated on one thing—I'm alone with my new husband. A guy who has fingered me to orgasm. A guy who I've blown. A guy I know almost nothing about despite our psychic connection. Heaving a huge internal sigh, I drag my head away from all things Tristan. It's hard enough to focus on my work with him in the room. I don't need the distraction from my fantasies.

I hide surreptitious glances at Tristan by clearing a space on the large desk and setting up my laptop. As I bend over a stack of journals to look at the elaborate calligraphy on the cover, I damned near head butt Tristan. He smiles down at me as he grabs my arms and steadies me.

I can feel the heat simmering deep within his core as a tangible thing. He doesn't hide the desire glowing in his eyes, and I drown in it while my mind goes into overdrive. *Down girl.* Seriously I have to work now. I haven't had a minute alone in ages, and I have a lot to think about. I'm an independent woman and this group dynamic may be too much. It's wonderful Troy is back but when I signed on, I didn't know he was a package deal to this extent. Do I want to be part of a quad for the long haul? I'm overwhelmed. Two mates and a third on the way. Can I do this harem thing? Do I want to do it? Cass and I had sex and now don't speak, Tristin is like a puppy underfoot, and Troy … Well who knows with all his sensitivities. Oh yeah, I so need a time out.

We stand that way for several hundred beats, staring, barely breathing. The sound of a throat clearing brings us back to planet Earth. Tristan leans close to my ear and murmurs, "Get your work done. I have plans for us." He gives my ass a playful slap, grabs a handful of the journals and settles himself in a comfy-looking leather armchair. I turn and meet Raphael's dark and inquiring gaze.

"Is there anything I can get you, Domina?" Raphael gives me another bow after setting a large tray on a sideboard.

"Please stop bowing to me, Raphael. You're not subservient to me. The keeper of the house's magic is a crucial position. I'm just a guest here," I say.

"You are the chosen one," Raphael says. "You have great power, and with great power comes great responsibility. I bow to show my respect."

I can't help doing a mental fist pump. I love the idea of being chosen. Somehow, it makes my recurring sci-fi dream about being a scientific experiment a little less psychotic.

There is something hugely different about me, but it's supernatural, not scientific.

"How about you save the bowing until we figure out what I'm chosen for. You may be a bit premature." I smile at him to take any sting out of the words.

Except I don't think he's offended by the gesture, merely curious. "If that's what you prefer, Domina. If that will be all?" He turns to leave and is halfway across the room before my latest mental-pause passes and my memory function returns.

"Raphael, is there WiFi and a printer available?"

He turns slowly and looks at me. "There is no connection to the outside world. As for printing, show me what you need, and I'll print it for you." He comes back to the desk and holds out his hand.

"It's on my computer." I open the digital workbook from my book study on my laptop and then show him the displayed values list. He studies it for a long moment then nods. "How soon do you need it, and how many copies?"

"Four copies, please. One for each of us. And—"

Tristan interrupts me. "Tomorrow morning will be fine, Raphael. Please ensure we're not disturbed this afternoon. *Domina* needs to get her work done." Tristan's firm tone brooks no argument. I snap my mouth shut and make busy on my computer while my traitorous libido argues with my need for independence. My lady bits seem to love this take-charge side to my new mate. Tristan starts leafing through the journals in his lap.

As the door snicks shut behind Raphael, I stare at this man, trying to decide whether I want to sink down on his hot shaft or give him a piece of my mind.

"You're staring, Ali. Is that a sign you've finished your work?" Tristan's searing gaze is no longer that of the guy next door. This is a man who knows what he wants and won't be shy about taking it.

Tristan's raw lust sends nervousness flooding through me. Despite my racy thoughts, I feel more like a teenager on her first date. I pretend it's a hot flash and fan myself with one hand. But that commanding voice inside my head compels me to make sure things are clear between us. "Tristan." At the sound of his name, that hot gaze snaps up to meet mine. Oh boy. "I prefer to speak for myself. Just because I think you're hot doesn't mean I've lost the ability to make decisions."

"Got it. So, you think I'm hot?" Tristan isn't at all perturbed by my assertiveness.

"That's one rabbit hole I'm not going down at the moment. I've got work to do." I hunch over my computer and get to work.

I have a deadline. I haven't missed a deadline in my life, and I'm not about to start now. I open the draft of my first article for Cyrus Stone. Within minutes, I'm immersed in the work and barely notice when Tristan brings me a sandwich and refreshes my tea.

When I'm satisfied with what I've written, I save the article and am about to open my email when I remember there's no Internet connection. *Piss.* I check my phone. No signal. I'll have to send it from the event tonight. I AirDrop the file to my phone, sigh and close my computer. Tristan's sitting in the armchair, hands tented under his chin, staring. At me. As if he's ready to consume me.

I have the instant need for a stiff drink as I gather my wits about me because it's feeling like a do-or-die moment. It doesn't matter that Tristan has already seen me naked. That had been in the forgiving dim light, and I hadn't been in my right mind. Now, we're in the cold light of day. I cross to a trolley laden with liquor, pour myself several ounces of decanted red wine and down it. Taking a deep breath, I turn and hold up the bottle. "Want some?"

"No." He crosses to the fireplace and touches a long match to the kindling below several logs sitting on a grate. Once lit, he tosses the match onto the logs and moves a large metal screen in front of the fire.

Oh boy. I pour several more ounces and turn around. Staring back at him over the rim of my glass, I sip my wine rather steadily and wait. Eventually, he'll say or do something to get this show on the road. Men always do when they want to get laid. But not this man.

He prowls over to the trolley and pours several fingers of something golden into a glass. Blue eyes smoldering with heat burn down on me as he takes a sip... And says nothing. Nope. After sending another flash of heat my way, he takes that gorgeous ass back to the fireplace and folds that perfect body onto one of the oversized floor pillows sitting on a beautiful Persian rug.

The pause gives me plenty of time to take inventory. I'm not exactly twenty anymore, and chronic illness and stress over Troy's illness have taken a toll. Maybe I can't even keep up with three guys. Who am I kidding here? What the hell have I gotten myself into?

Compared to a lot of women my age, I'm not in half bad shape. Okay, my rigorous exercise regimen followed the geese south when Troy got sick. I made a few half-hearted attempts to get back into it since, but it was just easier to take some THC and veg. I'd lost interest in pretty much everything I'd loved to do with Troy, including eating. On the bright side, I'd shed twenty excess pounds. With those pounds went most of the pot belly and reduced the big ass ... and my boobs, someplace I definitely could use a little more tissue. Not a lot. For the most part, I'd made peace with what nature gave me. After hearing the horror stories from my friends and watching their larger bosoms sag, I'd sent many silent prayers of thanks to the heavens for saving me from getting black eyes when I jog. I might not be willing to have a boob job, but there were times when I wouldn't reject an inch or two more. Or, at the very least, have them lifted back to the perky stage.

That thought no sooner forms in my head, when two things happen almost simultaneously. Something shifts in my boobs, and I could swear they're riding higher. But before I can make sure I'm not suffering from another menopause symptom, and I get a firm push from behind. *Get on with it.* I almost spill my wine as I lurch forward. The fucking house wants me to get it on.

Tristan's eyes remain fixed on me as if he's not sure what I'm feeling, so he'll wait for me to make the first move. I move my hand to push my glasses up and remember I've lost my shield. I take another hit of the wine, close my eyes, and focus on Tristan's chamber in my heart. A medley of emotion hits me—love, need, curiosity … and lots and lots of raw desire. I put down my glass.

"So, what are these plans of yours?" I start to move toward him.

"To get to know you."

"So, no sex?" I take several more steps and do something brazen. Something I've never done before. I pull off my hoodie and T-shirt while I keep advancing on him. He wants me. I can feel it. And for once in my life, I'm going to follow my instinct and do something spontaneous. Well, semi-spontaneous.

"Is that what you want with me? Sex?" The husk in his voice damn near makes me combust.

With you? Hell yes!

18

TRISTAN

My heart plummets as she regards me. I'm getting a strong message that she's having doubts. About me. About us. She'd made it clear I was in no position to speak for her, and I can't touch her without her permission. What if I'm all wrong about the connection between us?

When she hears I want to get to know her, something flares in her eyes. Her next words tell me she's disappointed.

"So, no sex?" She puts her wine down and comes toward me, pulling her hoodie and T-shirt over her head and tossing them on furniture she walks. Her jeans and panties follow before she steps out of her shoes and stands before me stark naked. She licks her lips as if getting ready to dive into a good meal. There's not a modicum of curiosity about who I am as a person.

The bubble I've been floating in bursts. I've been here before. I recognize the signs. Ali needs me as her boy toy, nothing more. Using the time it takes to stand, I bury that blossom of hope that had sprouted when our mating brand engaged. I'd wanted so badly to have a great love like Troy has with Ali that I'd refused to see the signs. Now that I know, my role is clear, and I know what needs to be done.

"Do you want sex? Because I'm happy to accommodate." Matching her movements, I rip off my T-shirt, displaying the full glory of my six-pack. When you add our angelic beauty to the sex angel charm, you get something few women can resist.

Ali hesitates a moment, and for a split second I think she realizes what I need, that she sees *me*. She places her tiny hands on my chest and kneads them slightly. I hold my breath, praying. When she reaches up and pulls my mouth to hers with hot demand, I lock my hope along with a healthy dose of hurt into a small chest and bury it deep within my psyche. I let go of love and slide into the snug fit of empty lust that's so familiar. She consumes my mouth for just a moment before I tear myself away. Despite my despair, every neuron in my body leaps to attention at the sight of her naked body. My erection springs free as my jeans drop to the floor.

I give her a moment to ogle me, my excitement for her on prominent display. I know two things for sure. I look damned good naked, and it's what women want from me. But Aleah has made it perfectly clear this is her rodeo, so I'm not going to make this easy. I stride over to the armchair and sit, letting my hard cock stand proud in invitation. She gives me a considering look.

"So let me get this straight. You're going to make me work for this?" She smiles to take the edge from the words. It doesn't work.

Oh yes babe, I sure as hell am. Women work to get a piece of this meat.

"Show me what you want." I fill my voice with quiet command. The pressure increases in the chamber of my heart where Ali's bond resides as she pokes and prods, trying to unearth my deepest secrets. But those walls are too thick for her to penetrate. Yet, I could swear that every time I strengthen the walls to block the onslaught of feeling spiraling through our mating bond, her indomitable willpower pushes back with equal force. But she's already shown me her truth of seeing me only as a sexual object, and she's right. Now that I've seen it, I can't ignore it.

A small cloud of doubt crosses Ali's face as she runs into my emotional walls. She gives a defiant shake of her head, tosses a throw pillow on the floor, and drops to her knees between my legs. For several long moments, she examines my junk as if she's looking at a rare gem while her fingers tickle the fine hairs on the inside of my thighs. She cups my balls in one hand and bounces her hand as if balancing their weight as she looks directly into my eyes. I return her stare with my best it's-only- sex look. She tosses back a small yeah-right smile as she grabs my shaft with her free hand and blows on the drop of precum oozing from the tip. My cock pulses in response. She gives it an extra squeeze before pulling the head into her wet mouth. I strain to suppress the reaction as my body begs to arch toward her, to let her claim me as her own. I could swear the chair groans as my grip crushes its arms.

As if she can feel my resistance, Ali plays my cock like a wind instrument using her lips, facial muscles, tongue, and teeth to tease every sensation known to humanity and a few that haven't been invented from me. She plays my organ at its full range combining air, tightening of cheek and jaw muscles as well as tongue manipulation until I'm panting with exertion from the sheer force of holding back my orgasm. My balls and anus tighten, waving the white flag of defeat.

With the fluid grace of a dancer, she rises from the floor, kneels over me, and swallows my throbbing cock with her molten cunt. She stills as another wave of contractions hits my balls and fences with my control. Three pulses go by before her hot sheath responds, tightening around and then releasing my throbbing cock. She holds her body upright, arms clasped behind her head, open to my hungry gaze, balancing her weight on her right knee and left foot with knees spread wide, wet lips engorged with her desire. We stay like this, suspended in time, until the urgent need to come passes, her eyes never leaving mine, the Nephilim glow trying to speak to me. The onslaught is worse than any siren's call urging me to succumb.

When she starts to move, her entire body becomes the instrument of my destruction. Her movements form a dance as she moves in time to some silent slow dance that slowly builds in intensity. She has superb muscle control and works me over with the athletic prowess of an Olympic athlete. If this were a competition, she would knock every one of the gods and goddesses off their thrones. The soft sheen of sweat covering her body draws my hands to her skin. I slide my hands over the smooth roundness of her belly and cup her breasts feeling the soft bounce against my palm as she performs athletic maneuvers on my cock. Her breasts pump in perfect rhythm with her cunt, like the two parts of a heartbeat, a heartbeat I desperately want to share.

I desperately try to hang onto my reserve, to keep that distance between us that will protect my heart. But I can't do it. I want Aleah to shatter all over me. I want to be the one who drives her past the point of just pleasure to oblivion with emotional connection. I want for one fucking minute to believe she wants me for more than my body.

I slide a hand between her legs and over her engorged clit, a rare pearl on display for my eyes alone. Ali lets out a low moan and slides forward until her face hovers over mine, supporting her weight with one hand on my shoulder. Our lips don't meet, but her breath mingles with mine as her eyes telegraph a message of hope, love, and light. I'm not fooled. It's my body she wants, not my mind. But I can't forget that glimpse of what could have been. I won't let her rip my heart out. I close my eyes.

"Tristan." Her low contralto is husky and raw.

I can't resist the pull to look at her.

"Tristan." Her breath blows the word over my heated skin. She cups the side of my face, and we have another moment while she holds my cock and my heart deep within her, refusing to let go. Maybe it's enough that she loves my beauty.

This time when she moves, she's insistent, demanding, pressing her clit into my finger. I increase the pressure and rub with short, deep strokes. She digs her fingers into my shoulders as she rides me fiercely. She's the most stunning woman I've ever seen. I roll her clit between two fingers. A low growl escapes, and I realize it's mine.

"I want you." Her thought slides along the channel that connects me to her. *"Make me yours."*

I answer with another deep rub of her clit. The strength of the contractions as her pulsing cunt clamps down around my cock makes me gasp. Her body shudders and shakes as her orgasm explodes from her. I grab the cheeks of her firm ass and push into her, driving my cock into the throbbing tissue of her G-spot. Another orgasm tears through her on the tails of the last. I grit my teeth with the exertion of holding back my explosion. My body becomes a machine, responding to hers, refusing to allow this moment to end.

But I can't make it last forever, so I give up and let go.

I try to stay lost in the moment, but a small hand playing with the fine hair around my nipple brings me back. It's an innocent enough gesture. And too intimate. If I stay here one more minute, I'll become a blubbering idiot begging her to *see* me. To love me. But sex angels don't blubber, and we certainly don't beg. And Troy's right about one thing: love can't be forced. Hurt wells within me along with the urgent need to run from the source. Ignoring the surprise on Ali's face when I lift her off, I use magic to put my clothes on as I head out the door. I can't think of anything to say, so I say nothing.

"Tristan." Her plea stops me at the door, and the hurt in her voice nearly tears my heart out but I don't turn around.

"Something's not right. I can feel it. It's like we're not friends anymore. Please talk to me."

And there it is, the "f" word. Friends. My heart breaks. I want her love, not her pity. I pull every shred of power in me to plaster a smile on my face and turn to face her.

"Of course we're friends. I'm just worried about tonight, babe. Troy and Cass need my help."

With that lame excuse, I walk away from the best and worst fuck of my life.

19

ALEAH

One instant, we're sitting, breath mingling, heartbeats in sync, and I'm coming down from one of the most mind-blowing orgasms of my life. Then Tristan damned near tosses my ass on the floor in his rush to get out of the room. Something is wrong, but like a pesky insect, the problem flits out of reach when I swat at it. I try to figure out what the hell went wrong. Tristan's pouty face is most definitely one way to kill post-orgasmic bliss.

Despite my best efforts to rationalize them away, my feelings are hurt … deeply. Tristan's the first guy I've been with since Troy and I became a thing. Fucking around is not something I do. Not that sex can't be just that, sex for sex's sake. It can. In theory. Just not for me. And forget about post-coital warm fuzzies because there sure as fuck weren't any today. I could swear the manor nods in agreement.

Another thought hits me, adding more weight to my distress. He didn't call me *mon chou.*

That doesn't matter. It's just a stupid pet name. My rational mind dukes it out with my emotions as I throw my clothes on and head to our bedroom to get ready for the big kink event tonight. I walk directly into the room-sized closet and start sifting through the clothes while deciding what to wear. In the emails I'd exchanged with the head dungeon monitor codenamed Maestro, he'd strongly suggested I wear black. It seems black and vinyl are the thing in the kink world.

"Well, that most certainly wasn't your finest hour. You're supposed to have the gifts of intuition and insight. Looks like we've got a lot more work than I expected to get you where you need to be."

I startle as Nye's voice sounds behind and above me. I look up, and there she is, floating above me in a seated position. Today, she looks as if she's about to attend a party in the nineteen twenties. She's sporting a silver dress with a very low neckline exposing loads of cleavage, two necklaces—one a choker and the other a double strand of white pearls, one elbow-length glove, and a headband. She taps what looks like a black carved chopstick against her bare palm.

"Awesome outfit." I'm about to ask a ghost if she's headed to a masquerade party and clamp my mouth shut.

"Right now, I'm the only thing keeping the spirits from thrashing poor Tristan and kicking his ass out of the manor, and if the manor rejects him, he won't be able to get back." Her pointed glare says this is all my fault.

"What on earth are you talking about?"

"The Druid gods have bound the power of these sacred grounds to you. That means the manor will respond to your feelings. It can feel you're unsettled. It thinks Tristan is the cause since this state overcame you after you had sex. The manor will respond by getting rid of anything that threatens you or makes you unhappy while you're in residence here."

Oh, for fuck's sake. If it's not one thing, it's another. I didn't sign on for all this nonsense. I push down the irritation starting to rise in me. I'm usually not this temperamental, must be my introverted nature. I haven't had a minute to figure anything out. And why does everyone always expect me to know what's going on?

Then what Nye said penetrates, and I look at her in horror.

"You were watching us?" Because one thing I know for damned sure is that I'm not into exhibitionism. My lady bits are not for public display. And if they were, it definitely wouldn't be for someone who could be my grandmother.

I quickly reassemble my face from horror to polite curiosity. After all, I'm not about judging or shaming. Plus, she's a ghost with magical powers and this is her house.

"No, I did not watch you. Voyeurism isn't my thing. Tristan passed me in the hall. I know a man who's been well fucked and then had his heart torn open. If I wasn't in this ghostly state, I tell you one thing. I might help the lad get over the tear in his beautiful heart. Poor boy." She thrusts her substantial chest forward, bringing to mind the erotic art surrounding us. Nye is definitely the woman in the living art. I close my eyes against the visual art inches from my face. One thing I don't need is a cougar role model. That's one image I'd rather not dwell on. Nothing to do with Nye, but I can't stand the idea of anyone fucking one of my guys. "And it wouldn't involve fucking." She looks thoughtful. "At least not to begin with," she adds as an afterthought.

"I don't mean to be rude, but why is the poor boy any of your business?" Yup, my hackles are rising. I hold a jumpsuit that has promise, but before I can examine it, something snatches it from my hand and puts it back on the rack. *"Not that one."* That strange echo of a voice sounds within me. Okie dokie, then. *"Listen up."*

"Because you are our business. These gods have named you the chosen, and you're protected by these sacred grounds and connected to their power. As the high priestess, I am the conduit between you and the magic, so think of it more as awareness than telepathy. Think of me as a mentor and guide." Nye's face frowns down at me in disapproval as if I'm her star pupil who has failed her entrance exam. "You're here because you need protection from that bastard Syrael while you get your wits about you. And you need to find, release, and learn to control your powers, am I right?"

Another nod. I'm starting to squirm under her direct gaze. Not liking where this discussion is heading, I turn my attention back to clothing selection. Her pointed statements phrased as questions don't fool me. I have been rather distracted with the guys instead of focusing on the threat to my life. She floats into my peripheral vision.

"The Rule of Three dictates there will be the third attempt on your life, and this one might be successful. That gives your situation some urgency. Would you agree?"

I give another reluctant nod. I knew I wasn't going to like where this was headed, but I resign myself to going along for the ride.

"And your point is?" My bitch goddess comes out of hiding and takes her gloves off.

The temperature in the room drops as the woman floats down to stand in front of me. Her ghostly visage jabs me with the ornamental chopstick. Ouch. I felt that.

"I have got a good mind to toss your backside back to Queen Hera. Maybe she can do something with your wilfulness. Let's see, shall we?" She tips her head back, and a needle of light shoots upwards. "Hera. A word."

The roof disappears, and the sky opens up. Suddenly, a low rumbling accompanies an electrical disturbance that sucks the air from the room. A moment later, a stunning older woman dressed in regal Grecian robes, wearing a crown, and holding a lotus-tipped scepter appears. Waves of power and the very pungent smell of lotus flowers hit me like physical blows as she frowns at me.

Nye smacks me with her chopstick and hisses a sharp, "Curtsy."

I hurriedly execute my best version of a deep curtsy before continuing to stare, stupefied.

Nye bows her head, then does an elaborate cheek kissing routine with the queen. Queen Hera steps back and looks at her.

"What brings me here, Anais? It's most unusual for you to summon me." I could swear the earth trembles as she says the word "summon," leaving no doubt that Nye better have a good explanation.

"You need to tell this young one to step up or appoint someone who will." Nye doesn't seem the least bit intimidated by this icon of shimmering power. My admiration turns to instant horror as her words penetrate. Wait just a fucking minute. I've been stepping up my whole life.

Both women direct the beam of their spotlight gazes my way, and I'm not feeling the fun.

"Oh?" Queen Hera lets the question hang in the air. She moves to a rack holding dresses and jumpsuits and starts shifting through it.

Nye joins her. "It's been over a week, and she has yet to assume her position and connect with her power. Two of her mates rejected her, and she's done nothing to protect or defend herself against Syrael. There's not much I can do with her until she's ready to accept her responsibilities."

Geez Louise. This Anais is one tough cookie. My shields go up faster than those on the Starship Enterprise.

"Don't be so hard on the child," Queen Hera says. She bestows another benevolent look at me ignoring the unmistakable frown I give her for referring to a middle-aged woman as a child. "What is holding you back from accepting your calling?"

What is holding me back? *What is holding me back?* My

internal screaming makes me instantly forget my argument about being a mature woman, and I stamp my metaphorical foot.. "I was minding my own business—"

"She means drowning her grief in a barrel of wine," Nye cuts in.

"When next thing you know, I'm possessed by the ghost of my dearly departed husband, find out he's a triplet and an angel, oh, and not just any kind of angel. No. My Troy has to be a sex angel and not one of the lowly kinds. He's a frigging sex angel lord. And if that wasn't enough, I find out I'm mated to at least one of his brothers and probably both."

"She's pouting because she just found out that a mating bond isn't an automatic guarantee of meaningful sex," Nye says.

I pointedly ignore her as my head of steam gains traction. I look at Hera and continue. "I've suffered through some kind of transition sickness, been poisoned by a vampire, and almost killed not once but twice. And all this with the vague notion that I'm some kind of chosen." I ball my fists and put them on my hips, fully caught up in self-defense.

"Well, aren't you hard done by?" Nye says. "Most would be thankful to be chosen by the gods. You don't question being chosen by the gods. You just do it."

"Do what? What precisely have I been chosen to do?" I let every bit of my frustration and self-pity bleed into my tone.

"You've been chosen to be an Erogelic Lord. In addition to your powers, you'll be able to use the power and traits of your divine mates. The prophecy says the chosen is the conduit for channeling that power. Only the combined power of the four of you will bring down Lord Syrael, but that is only a small part of your mission." Queen Hera pauses and shows Nye the black and sequined number she's holding. "This will do nicely." She hands me the outfit, and I drape it over the chair at the vanity.

I will not be distracted. My mission? I don't have any recollection of having accepted any mission. "What is the mission?"

"Love, compassion, and empathy should be the cornerstones of our societies, especially when it comes to sex. But sadly, our sex demons are using sex for evil and sin with the express purpose of humiliating and abusing people at a rate faster than our sex angels can control. The prophecy predicts that a Nephilim with incredible power will form a divine union with the three sex angel lords. Only their combined power will end the reign of the Demon Lord Syrael and his band of marauding demons. As the prophecy says, 'a Nephilim will rise from the depths of despair to lead them.' We believe you are that woman."

"Have you lost your mind? Have you talked to Cass? Does he look like the kind of guy who'd let himself be led by a woman?" I remember who I'm talking to and hastily add, "No disrespect intended."

A bolt of lightning shatters the clear sky. Queen Hera sighs and gathers her skirts. "Duty calls, child. Wear the jumpsuit tonight. You'll need it." With that pronouncement, she and the dense scent of lotus flowers vanish in another atmospheric disturbance that sucks the light from the room for several seconds.

"We have faith in you, child. You've been preparing for this your entire adult life. Now, it's time to apply what you've learned. Remember your strengths. Rumble with vulnerability." Queen Hera's words are clear in my mind.

"Now that that's settled, you need to understand what you did to that poor man's heart. When did you first sense there was a problem?" Nye carries on as if the queen hadn't been here.

I grab the reminder to rumble with vulnerability and hang on tight. How many women have their own personal ghost mentor who wields the power of the gods? She seems determined to give me the third degree. I give up all pretense of avoiding the subject and give her my full attention.

"We're here for you." There's that voice again, and I'm suddenly grateful for the help from these Druids, strange as it may be.

"Everything was fine. I did my work while Tristan read some journals. He'd said he had plans for us, and when I was done, I asked him what they were. He said he wanted to get to know me. Then, something possessed me and told me the best way for us to get to know each other was to make love." I pause, trying to figure out what the hell had happened next.

Nye nods. "Ah, so you jumped his bones, did you? Treated him like a prime cut of beef." Nye grins and pokes me with the chopstick. "It's clear as the nose on your face. The poor lad's suffering from PCD."

Where is Google when you need it? I search my brain for the acronym but come up with nothing. My ignorance must be what's evident on my face if her reaction is any indication. Her mouth quickly quirks to the right. She gives a massive eye roll and sighs.

"Post-coital dysphoria. He's depressed even though the sex was pleasant," Nye says. "He wanted to share something intrinsic, something emotional. You wanted to get your rocks off, and he was the handy object. It's PBS." My face must tell a story because she hastens to add, "Pretty Boy Syndrome."

Now it's my turn to look at Nye as if she needs her head read. I studied sexuality in university, and I've never heard of PCD. I bet Tristan's issue has more to do with me taking the initiative with these dominant types. "I don't think so, Nye. He could have spoken up any time. Guys hate it when women are assertive. Oh, he asked what I wanted, but he didn't want to know. When I didn't go all simpering idiot on him, his balls got in a knot." I ignore Nye, who's looking at me as if I'm the simpering idiot in this equation.

"Tristan's pain comes from a lack of love. Who initiated sex has nothing to do with it. It's all about the timing." Nye gives a sad shake of her head, then looks thoughtful. "I think that's it. I've been trying to figure out why the gods chose you. You're here to teach the boys about love."

How does one tell a high priestess of a magical manor that she's lost her fucking mind? Those dots don't connect. But as her words penetrate my armor, that new place of "knowing" inside me nods in agreement. My eyes had been opened to the soft core Troy's strength hid. I'd seen the same thing in Tristan. Fuck, I'd even talked to him about it. But I'd been so hot to have him, I'd ignored everything else. My ego makes one last weak attempt ignore the truth staring me in the face.

"They're sex angels, for the gods' sake. One would think they've got a degree in love. And what the fuck could I teach a sex angel about sex? I bet I can count the number of guys I've been with, and all but one were forgettable until Troy."

"I beg to disagree. Love brings a whole different flavor to sex. There's nothing that can compare with it. You of all people know that. You crushed that poor boy's heart." Nye grins at me wickedly. "I do want to hear more about this Nick of yours. Why do you think these beautiful men are drawn to you?" She picks the jumpsuit off the chair. "Let's get you dressed while we talk."

Before I can get a word out to ask when she'd read our diaries, my jeans, undies, and T-shirt are gone, and the black sequined jumpsuit's painted on me. The sleeveless top is cut away, showing my breasts' soft sides, and my nipples pop out like cherries topping a sundae. I'm not wearing any underwear, none at all.

"Perfect," Nye says.

"I'm not wearing a Kardashian castoff." Translation, I won't go to a sex event wearing a garment that's almost as revealing as if I were naked. What if I got excited? What if I leaked? That's a distinct possibility when I'm surrounded by all that sex. I reach up to undo the clasp and can't find one.

"Oh, and a frontal assault won't work with Tristan. When you figure out how you made him feel, you'll know what needs to be done. Good luck."

I turn just in time to see Nye snap her fingers and disappear. Great, just fucking great. Now I'm going to have to get Troy to help me figure out how to get out of this jumpsuit. I pause as I pass the mirror and take a look. Despite the round tummy and love handles, I look damned good. Maybe I should rethink this hasty decision.

2 0

ATROYEL

My breath almost stops ... again. When my beauty steps into the sitting room. It's not Aleah's external appearance that draws me. It's her inner beauty enhancing her exotic presence. Tristan gives a wolf whistle that he cuts off somewhat abruptly, earning him a sharp look from Cass. My eyes remain fixed on Aleah as I try to work out what's changed about her. She's wound up about something, and her emotions are too tangled to unravel at the moment.

The outfit she's wearing gives the caveman in me a sharp kick, and it's everything I can do to stop myself from leaping up and tearing the fabric away to reveal her naked body. Typically, I have firm control over my baser urges, but my cock decides now is a good time to revolt. Aleah gives me a small smile as she perches on the arm of my chair, but she ignores my hard-on and subtle efforts to shift into a more comfortable position. Her attention is fixed inward, and there's something on her mind. I put my hand on her back and slide my fingers into the slit in the fabric that runs down her spine. She takes my arm and moves my hand to her lap. She's not in the mood to play.

135

I squeeze her thigh to let her know I'm with her. "What's up, beauty? What happened?"

"I just got my ass kicked by Queen Hera," Aleah says. That statement brings Cass and Tristan to attention. Tristan downs his wine and leans forward, forearms on knees.

"The queen of the gods, Hera?" Tristan asks.

"Duh, who else. Use your head." Cass frowns at Tristan in his moody way, but it's Tristan's reaction that grabs my attention. Usually, he could give a shit what Cass has to say about him, but this time is different. Tristan's thoughts turn inward to a dark place I can't penetrate. If there's one thing I can't stand, it's bullying, and Cass often treads the border with Tristan. In the channel that's opened between us, I feel Aleah's penetrating focus switch to Cass.

"That was uncalled for, Cass, and I'm calling out that shaming behavior, and I'll explain why," she says. "If I were Tristan, the story I'd make up is that Cass thinks I'm stupid and doesn't value my opinion. I'd think I wasn't smart enough or good enough to have your love. I'd think—"

Cass explodes from his seat and stalks over to the chair I share with Aleah. "That's preposterous, Aleah, and quite frankly, we don't need you interfering in our business, divine mate or no divine mate."

Usually, this type of male aggression is a massive trigger for Aleah because of her abuse history, and I draw in a breath getting ready to take down my brother. Aleah surprises me. She stands and squares off with Cass.

"Don't you take that tone with me, mister." She jabs her index finger into his chest. "You may not like me, but I don't deserve that level of disrespect. Now, please sit down. I have something to say."

Raphael, a silent but consistent presence, takes that moment to glide into the room bearing a decanter of red wine and a glass on a tray. Aleah takes the glass he offers with a grateful smile and sits back on the arm of my chair. Cass puts his empty wine glass on the tray, stalks over to the trolley, pours himself a whiskey shot, and sits in a chair opposite Tristan. Raphael makes short work of refilling Tristan's glass and then mine before he leaves the room.

Aleah takes a sip of wine then cradles the base of the stem in her lap. "When Troy died, I lost a piece of my very soul. The story I told myself gathered despair with each passing day. I won't bore you with the details. Suffice it to say, it had to do with feelings of inadequacy, loneliness, and fear. Lots and lots of fear. All the fight left me, and I've been floundering ever since." She squeezes my hand.

"Then you three came and opened up a whole new world of magic, but there were strings—fight a demon lord, have three mates and take on some frigging undefined role as the chosen. So, I did what I do best and tried to control the uncontrollable when what I need to do is have faith, to go into this with no guarantee of the outcome. I have to stop controlling and predicting and let nature take its course." Aleah stops and looks at each of us for several beats. "I need to rewrite the story about not being good enough, so that's what I'm going to do. I am worthy of love and connection. I think whatever I'm called to do has something to do with that. First, I'm going to remind myself of what I love about me, and then I'm going to love you all with my whole heart even though there's no guarantee with you two." She smiles at Tristan and Cass. I sit quietly as usual but inside, I'm brimming with pride. I do love this woman.

"To answer your question, Tristan, it was Queen Hera. At least that's who Nye called her," Aleah continues.

"Who the fuck is Nye?" Cass doesn't do well with women in positions of power. Sadly, my brother is a bit of a male chauvinist, and I'm not at all surprised Aleah's taking him in hand. I'd been waiting for it to happen. The strong, determined, take no shit from anyone woman I love is back, and it's sexy as hell. She gives him a penetrating look until his body language relaxes.

"Nye is what I call the owner of this house and the high priestess of this forest, which is sacred Druid ceremonial grounds. Her name is Anais Blackstone," Aleah says. "She wants to be called Lady B or Nye."

"The woman who wrote the journals," Tristan says in a quiet voice. Aleah's attention flits to him for a second, and I wait for her to ask about the journals, but she doesn't. Surprised by her restraint, I grab her hand and squeeze it for support. She squeezes back but doesn't look my way.

"As you probably gathered yesterday, Nye is a ghost, and it seems only Raphael and me can see her. She's been appointed by the gods to be my mentor and coach, and she's somewhat pissed at my lack of commitment. Nye called Queen Hera, who read me the riot act about being the chosen. She basically told me to start cooking or get out of the kitchen," Aleah says.

I sense Aleah's leaving something out of the story and make a note to ask her about it later.

"She told you to shit or get off the pot, and you decided to take a shit," Cass says.

Aleah grimaces, and her inward flinch works its way along our channel. For some reason, I never found out why, she can't stand hearing some swear words used in context, and shit tops the list. "I wouldn't have put it so graphically, but yes."

"What does that mean for us?" Tristan asks. The wall he's put up prevents me from getting a read off him, but there's no doubt something's bothering him that has to do with Aleah.

Care and concern for Tristan flood through our connection as she regards my brother, and I can't help but wonder what the hell happened between the two of them this afternoon. Whatever it is seems to have charted them into troubled waters. Since Aleah can't stand interpersonal discord, those cards will be laid on the table in short order, and I'm quite willing to watch. My beauty's strutting her stuff.

"I can't say what it means for you, but I can tell you what it means for me. We're tied together in this, so we'll have to find a way to work together to defeat Lord Syrael. Other than that, I'm not sure. Queen Hera confirmed what some of us suspected, that all three of you are my divine mates," Aleah says. Cass opens his mouth. Aleah puts up the hand holding mine, and a small pulse of power shoots through the air. Cass's mouth snaps shut, and he doesn't look the least bit pleased about it.

"I have the floor. Your turn will come." She takes a sip of wine and keeps her gaze trained on Cass, seemingly unaware of her power. "I realize you reject the notion of being mated to me out of hand, but if we're going to get through this alive, we're going to have to figure out how to work together." She looks at Tristan and gives a sad little smile. "I have no idea what I did to offend you today, and I assure you it was inadvertent, but I get that something's changed." She takes the hand I'm holding and puts it over her heart. "I can feel it here." I get the hand back. "That makes me sad, it truly does, but I honor your feelings. I won't force myself on you."

Tristan gives a curt nod but says nothing.

Aleah squeezes my hand, rises, and starts pacing, the globes of her firm ass moving seductively under the tight fabric covering them.

"From what I can gather, the house and grounds are lending me their power while I figure out mine. I have no idea what my powers are, and *I* have to discover them according to the prophecy. What I do know is that the angel of death, Nye, and now Queen Hera all say I've been in training for this role most of my life. Queen Hera reminded me of something just before she left that leads me to believe my powers have something to do with empathy and vulnerability," she says.

As if on cue, Raphael chooses that moment to drift in and refresh her wine. "Perhaps Domina's mates can lend some insight into your strengths. Sometimes loved ones see things in us we don't see ourselves."

Cass bristles, and Aleah throws him a warning glance. "Good point, Raphael. What is my superpower?"

"Command Brain, without a doubt," I say.

"Babe, that's not a superpower," Aleah says. "I don't think the ability to lean into uncomfortable conversations is a superpower."

"I beg to differ." Raphael's tone is respectful, but there's more to this caretaker than meets the eye. "Supreme Voice often referred to as Absolute Command, is one of the absolute divine powers."

"So, if I have this power, what can I do?" Aleah's in full skeptic mode now.

"If you have the divine power, you can use your voice to command and create anything and everything. Divine users can manifest their voice anywhere. Lesser users may be restricted to commanding their creations or living things. The strength of your power will be evidence of your divinity," Raphael says.

"I don't think so," Aleah says. Tiny pulses of power travel through our connection as she paces. A wicked grin transforms her face. "I'll prove it to you." She turns and wiggles her index finger in the general direction of my crotch. "Tickle Troy's balls."

I have trouble repressing my reaction as a tingling sensation starts deep in my balls. It's weak, but it's definitely there. *Godsdamn.* I grab Aleah's wrist. "Seriously, beauty? You choose tickling my balls for your first magical act?"

Aleah grins. "What were you expecting? Let me guess, that I'd solve world hunger or something equally lofty, right?" She gives me an exaggerated eye roll. "I think I'll perfect my skill, first."

She turns in Cass's direction. "Cass, get a hard-on for me." She stares at Cass's crotch as the pulse of power leaves her.

Cass blocks it just in time, but not before I feel the twitch of his cock.

"Feel anything?"

"Not a thing."

Cass's blasé tone doesn't fool me for a second. *"Liar."*

"Fuck off." From Cass.

Aleah turns to Tristan and does the finger thing. My beauty watches too many epic fantasy shows. "Tristan, please forgive me."

This time, I feel the pulse of her power on an emotional level. Our connection tells me that Tristan feels her power to a lesser degree, probably because his wall is up, but I feel him push back.

"Whatever it is you're trying to do isn't working," Tristan says.

She turns to Raphael. "Told you."

"Perhaps we should keep trying," the old man suggests. "Try thinking the words instead of speaking them."

She turns to me. "Your turn."

I stand and cross to her before she can react. "Grab your stuff. It's time to go. You've got work to do."

Raphael steps forward with a small vial. He pulls a cork from the top and hands the bottle to Aleah. "Drink this. It will cover random or inadvertent bursts of magic. However, any sustained bursts of power will break through the protection from this spell."

Aleah takes a whiff of the bottle, wrinkles her nose, then downs the contents. "Ahhh. That stuff's vile."

She grabs her wine and downs it while Raphael hands each of us a pandemic mask. "You'll need these to blend in with the natives."

Although she halts the habitual action of pushing her glasses in place, it's not before I see the tell. She's nervous, excited, and ready to get this show on the road. She gives me a warm smile and lets her small hand drop to my forearm for several long, comforting moments. We take a moment. Then, I slap her ass, open a portal and step into the lobby of the Acquired Taste club.

21

TRISTAN

As soon as we all assemble in a dark corner of the sex club parking lot and shake off the transition, Cass says, "Listen up. Here's the plan."

"Oh no you don't, Cass. This is my party, and I'll do what I want. I'm gathering material for my article, and I need to be free to roam where the spirit takes me. Besides, that dreadful potion that Raphael gave me will cloak any bursts of magic that might break free from me, right?" Ali turns toward the club as if the subject is closed. The beginnings of an apoplectic fit rumble in Cass's core. A little surprising since he claims to be immune to her. It appears Ali's giving him grief too.

Cass turns to Troy. "Do something about this, would you? We're walking into a potentially dangerous situation that calls for a defensive strategy. We need to—"

"We'll be fine, Cass," Troy cuts in. "We've already done reconnaissance, and we know the layout. I'm with Aleah on this one. I'll be close, and you two will sense if anything's wrong. Go enjoy yourself."

Cass glowers at Troy, but there's not much he can say.

Troy is tough to argue with when he gets logical, and it seems that Ali swims in the same analysis loving pool. Cass would be no match for both of them.

"You make it sound as if we're free to go play," Cass says.

"Sure. Why not? What's stopping you?" Troy sounds curious, as if trying to figure out a formula that doesn't make sense. Troy can sense that Cass and I are disturbed. The longer he connects with us again after the twenty-five-year absence, the stronger the signal gets, but for now, it's vague. From Troy's perspective, Cass is a free agent. Hell, Troy probably thinks we both are. Fundamentally, Troy believes that people should do what they genuinely wish as long as it doesn't hurt someone else. Comically, he struggles with the same perspective when it comes to Ali, despite his protests. But whatever's going on with Cass is too entertaining for me to give that much thought now. And it's a terrific distraction from thinking about my situation with Ali. There's not much Cass can say in response to Troy's question unless he wants these two to help him examine his feelings. Something we're not very good at. We're great at figuring out what other people are feeling; that's our job. We hate looking at ourselves. That's too much hard work.

Ali steps forward, concern written all over her lovely face. *Too late.* "What's upsetting you so much?" she asks Cass.

Cass's expression turns a shade darker. "Not a fucking thing. If you two figure you've got things under control, who am I to stop you? Let's go, Tristan." Cass stalks off in the direction of the club. I glance at Troy. Ali steps forward as if to touch me, and I step away, following Cass. I'm too vulnerable to let her touch me. Being near her tears at something inside me, and I've learned to protect myself from that kind of hurt. Block the pain.

I take out my phone, thankful for the strong signal. After sending the article to Daisy, I scroll through several text messages, most of them from her. I'll have to connect with her in person very soon or jeopardize our working relationship, and I don't want that whatever this new situation.

After we get through the entrance screening by presenting the confirmation numbers Ali got from her magazine, we sign the required rules and confidentiality forms. Cass stalks into the venue and leads me to the main play area. Troy and Ali follow a few minutes later, and I'm acutely aware of her presence. They stop just inside the entrance and look around the room, heads bent together, whispering. Troy is happy and at peace for the first time since our carefree childhood before losing our parents in the great war. Something fundamental within him has changed due to Ali's love and care during our separation. I wrestle with a twinge of some emotion I can't identify—jealousy? Envy? Longing? I turn off that tap. I don't want to face what this awareness might reveal.

Impact play stations line the walls of the large room with the requisite fifteen feet between each station to allow room for onlookers. The roped-off stations include several spanking benches, three St. Andrew's crosses, suspension rigs, raised circular tables with revolving tops. Two stations hold nothing but rubber mats. Once a scene is in play, patrons aren't allowed inside the ropes.

Several patrons line up in front of a woman dressed in Goth garb and wearing a mask adorned with a large lipstick-lined open mouth sucking a cock. She sits at a table near the entrance with a large flip chart beside her where she records names on an appointment sheet marked off in forty-five-minute increments. Until play begins, we're free to wander and check out the equipment as long as we didn't touch anything without permission. Troy and Cass's reconnaissance allows Troy to act as a tour guide, and he points out a few of the stations. Ali asks a few questions before approaching the scene sign-up monitor. After a minute or so of animated conversation, she nods and moves away.

No matter how hard I try, I can't completely shut down the sense of her presence. I can't stop comparing her to the women swarming this club despite the pandemic. As usual, many patrons, males and females alike, eye me up and down, assessing how to get a piece of this tasty morsel. Not one of them raises even a remote flicker of interest from my libido, and I ignore the looks.

I follow Cass around as he checks out the stations, uncharacteristically undecided about where he wants to start tonight's play. After several minutes of trying to convince myself I'm not interested in what Ali's doing, I realize I'm going about this all wrong. Ali had stomped on my heart in a way I hadn't expected. We'd shared that moment when I'd lain my soul bare in a way I hadn't done with another being, not even my brothers. I'd trusted her with my deepest secret, and she'd betrayed my trust.

Maybe Cass is right. Maybe she's here with some ulterior motive. If that's the case, then I'd be better to stay close and try to figure out what she's up to. Ignoring that annoying voice inside me that's jumping up and down, waving red flags about what possible motive Ali might have, I make my way over to the spanking bench. Ali is having an animated discussion with a Domme while pointing to the purple-assed sub strapped to the bench. As I edge closer, I hear her say, "I'm researching for a series of articles on the lifestyle. May I ask your sub a couple of questions?"

The Domme nods while she rubs and squeezes her sub's ass. Ali moves to the head of the bench and crouches down beside the sub, a large woman with tears running down her face. "May I ask you about your experience?" Ali's voice is low, respectful, and she's sexy as hell as her ass cheeks push out of that damned jumpsuit. I'd have much preferred her wearing those sweats she's so fond of, although pretty much anything she wears is a distraction. *Stop wanting her!*

The sub turns her head and waits for her Domme's nod of approval before looking back at Ali and nodding.

"Do you like pain?" Ali asks. Talk about cutting to the chase. Both the Domme and sub seem surprised by the blunt question. Ali, like any good interviewer, watches her closely and waits for her answer. Troy wanders around the space looking at the display of spanking implements, but I can't take my eyes off Ali.

The sub shakes her head in response to Ali's question. Ali cocks her head for a moment, then asks, "Why do you like being spanked?"

"It pleases my mistress," the sub replies. "She knows what's best for me."

I don't need our connection to know what's going on in Ali's head as the sub makes this pronouncement. I've known her long enough to know that she doesn't understand why someone would want to give away control. She isn't judging. The concept is so far from her values, and she struggles to get her head around it. After a few moments, she thanks the sub and moves on. After questioning a few patrons setting up impact stations, we approach a group that's gathered waiting for a scene to start. There's a low buzz of gossip, and a weird vibe comes from the men with the frequent mention of someone called BallBurn. I follow Ali and Troy as she works her way into the crowd. She stops in front of a large man with massive forearms crossed over an equally massive chest.

"Hi. Remember me? We met at…" Ali waves her hands in the air, careful not to mention any names. The man unfolds those arms, biceps popping all over the place as he lifts her into the air.

"Of course I remember you, sweetheart. Good to see you. I was wondering if we'd cross paths again. Are you here to play tonight? I'd love to spank that ass of yours." The man continues to hold her about a foot off the ground. It's evident as they talk that they've only met once before at an event in Canada when she researched submissives. Troy looks on in amusement as he watches her. I sidle up beside him as Ali gets the guy named Art to put her down and asks him to explain the upcoming scene with this BallBurn—a masochist who gets off on challenging women to kick him in the balls. Not my kink and mild compared to what I've seen as a sex angel, but Ali is fascinated by what would motivate a man "to invite pain men describe as horrific" solicits opinions from Art and his buddies.

"Does she accost people like this often?" I ask.

"All the time," Troy says. "You'll get used to it. She's got an inquiring brain. You haven't lived until you've witnessed her cougar attacks. She randomly picks hunks and talks to them about whether they realize they could be a model for GQ Magazine or a hero in a romance novel. Their stunned reactions give her fodder for the blog she writes called *Cougar Chronicles*."

"Don't you worry about her putting herself in danger?"

"Sometimes," Troy admits, "but I've learned she has excellent intuition about whether there's any threat to her. She's not susceptible to false flattery, and her radar is high tonight. As is mine. With Ali, I remain vigilant in the background and hope for the best."

"Sounds like one hell of a way to live," I say.

"I'm never bored," Troy says as BallBurn steps onto a large rubber mat signaling the scene is about to start. Dressed as if he's a gladiator with leather straps crisscrossed over his chest and a loincloth, he stands, legs spread shoulder-width apart. Conversation stills, and the group takes a collective breath as a tall, willowy blond woman wearing a sleeveless vinyl suit joins him in the ring.

"That's Eden."

"She'll take him down."

A barefooted Eden slinks to BallBurn with long, exaggerated steps, circling him while watching him with the eyes of a predator. She stops in front of him and tosses back a long ponytail before mirroring his stance. "How much are we looking for tonight?"

"Give me the full treatment," BallBurn says.

Eden links her fingers and stretches her arms before taking a few steps back and bracing her feet on the mat. She follows a couple of running steps with a sharp kick to BallBurn's testicles. The balls of every guy in the group collectively contract as Eden's shinbone connects with his package. He barely winces and shrugs, grinning at Eden. "Is that all you've got?"

Ali's watches open-mouthed as Eden repeatedly batters his balls with her shin. Ten or twelve kicks later, the blunt force still hasn't brought him to his knees. BallBurn openly taunts Eden as she circles him once again. "Looks like you're not woman enough to bring me down."

"Be careful what you're asking for." Eden does another lap around him.

"Bring it on," BallBurn says.

The guys around me hum in horror as Eden flexes and points her feet before resuming her battle stance. Every one of us holds our breath as she hauls off and kicks him in the balls. Hard. The sharp force from her foot drops him to his knees. The pain reverberating through him almost brings me to mine. I focus on BallBurn's emotional output. He's content on many levels. He can engage in rough play freely without judgment, and he's experiencing a high similar to of athletes when they push their bodies to the limit.

"What does he get out of this?" Ali asks.

"It's the sudden rush of pain that turns him on," Troy says. "Some people need serious pain for sexual excitement."

Baffled, Ali shakes her head and maneuvers out of the small crowd. When she steps into clear space, she stops, looking around until she spies a Domme flogging a naked man strapped to a St. Andrew's cross. Ali steps close to the rope barrier and watches with fascination as the woman uses one then two floggers to work over the slave. Using muscular arms, the Domme lifts the man's semi-erect cock and flogs his balls with gusto. The harder the Domme whips, the harder the slave gets. By the end of the scene, he's sporting a raging boner. Ali makes a few notes and walks away while the Domme administers aftercare, massaging the slave's swollen balls. Not my scene, but lots get off on it. Clearly, Ali's baffled, but she remains curious.

Troy and I trail behind her as she pauses briefly to watch several patrons scattered around a raised, revolving circular table bearing a naked woman on all fours. Laughter and quiet cheers greet us as they treat the woman to a birthday spanking game.

"It all seems like a lot of performance art," Ali says to Troy. "It's not about sex." She seems mystified by this discovery.

"Theater is an apt comparison, beauty." Trust Troy to be academic about the whole thing. "The BDSM lifestyle often involves costumes, props and role plays, but I'd say it takes performance art to a whole other level."

"I get the sense that some of these folks have trouble separating the scene from reality," Ali says. Despite the block I have in place, I could swear I feel a pulse of power coming from her as she surveys the room.

"The lines are blurred in many cases," Troy says. He squeezes the back of her neck, and the two exchange a caring smile that makes my heart twist.

I don't care. I won't care. I hope it won't take long for my heart to catch up with my brain.

Ali drifts toward the sensation playroom and stops dead just inside the door. She grabs Troy's arm and stage whispers, "Can you feel that? Someone is scared to death."

Ali's no doubt referring to the waves of fear coming at us from somewhere in the room. Standing behind Ali and Troy so that the three of us form a tight triangle, I scan the room looking for the source of the fear. Ali's sharp intake of breath draws my attention to a spanking chair set tucked into the corner between the wax and fire play tables. Cass's back is to us as he alternately spanks, caresses and whispers to a voluptuous woman whose ass is prominently displayed for our viewing pleasure.

22

ALEAH

Fear from the crowd damned near takes me out at the knees as security lets us into the club. There's so much of it I can't tell who it's coming from. It sits there, a low hum, a presence of its own, and I gradually get used to the feeling as Troy and I make the rounds in the impact playroom. I love having Troy as my encyclopedia of sex, and he manages to weave foreplay into our exchanges while still respecting our need to work. God, how I love this man.

Similar to what I experienced at the kink event I'd attended last year, the club's emotionally charged without feeling the least bit sexual despite the nakedness and sex toys prominently displayed at each station. After taking stock of the layout, I approach an attractive woman dressed in one of the coolest Goth outfits I've ever seen. She's sitting beside a flip chart set up on an easel, having an animated conversation with a short man leading a woman wearing nothing but a dog collar attached to a leash. I try to figure out what's different about the woman as I wait my turn and realize that she hasn't got another strand of hair other than what's on her head. Not anywhere. It's as if she's been waxed from head to toe. Even her eyebrows are gone.

"It's called epilation," Troy murmurs in my ear. I make a mental note of the term. Tonight's all about the experience. There'll be plenty of time to research my findings later.

As the couple steps away, the Goth writes in one of the boxes on the flip chart paper before resuming her seat. She jiggles the many bracelets that she wears over her fingerless gloves. "Time and station." She puts down the marker and looks up at me. I go into my spiel about researching an article making sure I drop her boss's name and find out that each patron reserves a station for a forty-five-minute scene. That leaves fifteen minutes for clean-up before the next scene.

Next, I start a systematic tour of the room, starting with the first spanking station. I knew from my previous experience that I could examine the stations before the scenes started as long as I asked for permission before touching any toys or addressing any subs or slaves. The whole concept of slavery being a choice brings mixed feelings, but I had a better understanding of why someone might choose to be a slave after interviewing Slave Kitten last year. I'd began our interview with more than a hint of scepticism and, dare I say, judgment in my heart. No fucking way anyone would choose to be dominated by a man twenty-four-seven. It took less then half and hour into her story for me to be absolutely convinced living the lifestyle had been her choice and without it, she'd be dead.

I try not to personalize while I watch a Domme spank her slave at the first station. Each blow that lands on the slave's ass reverberates through mine, reminding me of when Cass took me over his knee. Each smack of the paddle makes me yearn for the burn from Tristan's hands on my ass. Troy's hand squeezing the back of my neck reminds me we have plenty of time for my sexy thoughts later. Right now, I have work to do.

I make the rounds, sprinkling my questions equally between Dominants and submissives. Troy proves to be a font of knowledge he's happy to share. We linger at the caning station while Troy and the Dom exchange information faster than I can get it down. "Use a cane made from rattan that's flexible. It can break, so check for slivers. Measure so it doesn't wrap around the thighs. Hit low and hold to hit the sweet spot. Can bring women to orgasm if cane held so vibrations can have time to work."

I highly doubt this last piece of information as I jot it down and remind myself I'm not here to be critical. **YKIN-MKBYKIOK** signs adorn the walls reminding us that "your kink is not my kink, but your kink is okay."

Troy and the Dom finish up with an animated discussion of how to measure a butt while I wander over to a suspension harness station.

"I prefer the cross." Troy cups an ass cheek as he comes up behind me and whispers in my ear. I shudder with anticipation as we hold a hot glance for several beats. Unlike whatever the fuck's going on with the other guys, nothing stands in the way of Troy and me celebrating our love. We speak the unspeakable with our bodies. The heat in his eyes promises I'll be begging for him to stop before he's done with me. He grips the back of my neck in that possessive way I love and brushes his lips over mine. We can wait. I smile in answer as he straightens, offering another prayer of gratitude to the universe for sending me this man.

He was more than man enough to step aside and let me run my show, knowing his time would come. Troy's love is a gift on so many levels bringing joy I wish the world could share. Despite the intense pain I'd suffered during his death and dying, I'd do it all again to experience a moment of the joy we had. Tristan comes up behind us, breaking the moment. I push away the twinge of pain that comes when I glance at Tristan and get back to work. There'll be time to think about that later.

I watch with fascinated horror as the guy calling himself BallBurn gets ready to let someone kick the crap out of his genitals. Questions whip through my mind as I realize I'm sensing the collective horror of the men clumped around the kicking station. I shake off low-level nausea as they imagine the pain and threat of permanent damage from a hard kick to the balls. Something about this place has put my intuition on hyperdrive. Reaching within, I let my instincts guide me. I'm picking up on the emotions of people around me. That in and of itself isn't new. I've reacted physically to the stress or tension in a room for as long as I can remember. But this is different. Stronger. With these men, I can identify the emotions flowing through them. Some are appalled—*no fucking way would I let someone kick me in the nuts, never mind asking for it*. Some hid disgust. All had experienced some degree of nausea as each blow hit home. And I'd felt it.

Can cocks fracture? I'm sure I'd heard they could. *Could they get a hard-on while suffering intense pain?* There are so many questions that never came up during my sexuality studies in university. I hide a smile as I imagine my profs clasping their hands and sending a prayer of thanks to the universe. They'd had more than enough of my "interesting" questions but not one of them topped the question that had stunned my grade twelve biology teacher speechless. "Why does our frog have such a big penis?"

After a protracted discussion, the "penis" had turned out to be a stomach flap. I'd faked being mortified at my mistake to hide my delight at having discovered a topic that puts adults into a tailspin. Not much has changed when it comes to the subject of sex. They may have gotten worse. We millennials are too stressed, leaving too little time or energy for the fun things in life, like sex. It's one of the reasons Troy and I had debated whether we wanted kids. Before the universe decided for us.

When BallBurn finally drops to his knees after twenty or thirty kicks, nausea builds. I'm definitely reacting to the emotion coming from the men around me. The urge to flee overwhelms me, and I wrestle my way through the group muttering repeated excuse mes. After I break free, I find a relatively empty spot behind a spanking table of some sort and catch my breath. Troy waits quietly beside me, no doubt assuming I'm doing more research.

Whatever's happening inside me relates to my nearness to the source. Back here in my quiet corner, the emotional assault recedes to the low buzz I'd felt when we arrived. Something in the next room flickers at the edge of my awareness, and I head toward it. Fear slams into me the moment I cross the threshold at the exact moment I set eyes on Cass, his hand sliding between the very naked thighs of a gorgeous woman. For a split second, I think I'm reacting to seeing Cass but quickly realize I'm feeling someone else's fear. I thank the gods for the wall behind me as I lean against it and absorb the pain seeping through me. It's as if I'm a small child huddled in terror. Dry sobs of despair tear through me as I wait for the pain to start again.

All senses go on high alert. Someone's in trouble, someone young. I need to find the child and assess the risk. Darkness mingles with the fear snapping all three of us to attention.

"Be on guard," Troy hisses. "Act natural. Tristan, alert Cass. I'll check out the other room." He squeezes my hand. "Stay here. I'll be right back." He uses our connection to let me know my guys will protect my back.

I tighten my grip on his hand. I'll be okay. The inner

voice barking orders inside me tells me it's crucial to act naturally. I step closer to the wax play station, ask a few cursory questions and move on. I skirt around the corner where Tristan's large frame blocks my view of Cass's body and stop at the fire station. Now the fear hits me like blows, and it takes all my willpower to appear interested as a large woman wipes a small area of very hairy skin with a wet cloth before lighting the area on fire. Keeping my eyes trained on the activity, I dig through the fear to a tiny voice repeating the word no. I step around the table until the fear grows. It seems to be coming from a dark corner in the L-shaped room. I edge toward it, stopping every step to read the situation. A black couch sitting against the far wall beckons, and I drop onto it. The fear spikes at the exact nanosecond I see the cage sitting in the corner. It's covered with a black cloth making it almost invisible. But whoever dropped the cloth missed a corner, and I swear I see a small, dirty foot snatch away. Fear vaults to terror that makes my windpipe constrict. I close my eyes and force myself to relax and breathe through the panic.

"Don't talk to me. Don't talk to me." The small voice screams the words over and over inside my mind. It's a fucking strange sensation, but I don't have the time to analyze it right now. I've got to find out what's making this child so afraid and right quick. Then the dots connect. A child. No fucking way should a child be at an event like this and most certainly not in a cage.

"Why not?" I send the message telepathically, answering the small voice.

"He'll see us. Go away. Leave me alone."

"No one can see me talking to you. I'm wearing a jockstrap on my face. Have a look. Besides, I'm not talking to you. You're reading my thoughts. My name is Aleah. What's your name?"

There's a long pause before I see two eyes gleaming in the

dark, reminding me of a trapped animal. I need to gain a measure of trust and fast.

"Tommy. If he catches you, he'll beat you." His voice in my head is thready, but there's a hint of courage there. *"I'm not worth saving. He says so. You can't save me. No one can."* The resignation in his voice breaks my heart, and it suddenly becomes very personal for me. I'd been that child who reached out for a lifeline that no one threw. I know the pain and despair of believing no one's willing to save me because I'm worthless. This child will not be lost on my watch. The annoying hum inside me increases as waves of hot flashes roll through me. Great. Not the best time for a menopause attack. With the heat comes the certainty that I know how to help this boy.

"Don't you worry about me. I had a dream that a boy like you was going to help save us. See this big guy sitting beside me? He's one of my friends. The other two are around the corner. We need your help."

"What can I do? I can't walk. I can't do anything." Tommy's curiosity overcomes his fear, a good sign.

Troy comes back. After one long, penetrating look, he sits beside me, his calm alpha-male poise belying his careful attention as he scans the room. I open the connection between us and beam him a message. *"I'm going to heal that child. He can't walk, so we'll need to carry him."*

Troy receives the message and lets me know he'll alert Cass and Tristan to be on the ready. He heads in their direction as I crouch to examine the cage, fighting the rise in Tommy's terror. I'm fiddling with the lock on the cage, muttering "open sesame" and the like when a viselike grip clutches my neck and lifts me in the air. The arm holding me curves bringing me nose to nose with dark, evil eyes in a handsome face devoid of humanity. Two small teardrop tattoos near his left eye tell me all I need to know—this man is a killer. The smell of his cheap cologne and the stench of body odor triggers something deep inside me, but this time it's certainty instead of terror. *This will not happen again.* Power surged through me, along with confidence bordering on cockiness.

"How dare you touch my slave?" Killer doesn't show one shred of fear or remorse for having brought a kidnapped child to a public event. Why would Cyrus Stone send me to an event so clearly connected to the criminal element?

"I'm going to ask you once nicely. After that, I won't be responsible for my actions. Put me down. You've got five seconds." I'm a firm believer in fairness and giving folks a second chance, but I'm not the slightest bit dismayed when his rage grows and hardens.

He tightens the grip on my neck. "You little bitch—"

Anger explodes out of me. *I'm not going to take abuse anymore.* The thought no sooner enters my mind, and Killer's body slams against the wall. Glowing strands lash his wrists and ankles to invisible hooks holding him suspended. All hell breaks out in the room around me. Several large guys are trying to break through to help the screaming man on the wall. "Oh no you don't." All four men fly backward as I utter the words. "Shields up." Suddenly, I'm Jean-Luc Picard commanding the Starship Enterprise. A shimmering barrier of light drops between the crowd and me and the child.

"I can't look. He'll make me hurt so bad. No. No." Tommy's mental screams rip through my head.

"Tommy, stop." I put extra firmness into my mental command. *"Watch me."*

As Tommy's hysteria calms, I turn back to Killer, who continues to hurl every disparaging name he can think of. The mist rising from my palm gives me an idea. I look back at the man wiggling on the wall like a human starfish and cup my hand as if squeezing his sac. Killer screams and pants for breath as the pain takes hold. I take a step closer to him.

"You like names, well here's one for you. Son of Satan. We'll call you SS for short." I stretch my arm toward him to help me direct the power flowing from me. "From this day forth, SS, you will suffer the consequences of your evil actions. Every time you think of abusing another living being, you will suffer the emotional and physical pain you inflicted on one of your victims. If you intentionally hurt another living being emotionally, physically, or sexually, you will suffer incapacitating stomach and bowel spasms for three hours."

That should do it. I dust my hands together. Not bad for my first try with my power. The sense of Tommy's fear turning to hope brings me back to the club and the chaos whirling around me. My guys hold back Killer's crew, but the spell hiding me disintegrates under our sustained magic. The power's burning up in me, but I have the feeling I don't have long left. I hustle over to the cage. This time as I think the words, 'open sesame,' the cage springs open. I hunker down and peer at the filthy child huddled in the corner. I inhale a deep calming breath and ignore my churning stomach as I hold out my hand. Light glows through the blue-white mist rising from my hands. Tommy's instant terror pushes back the tiny flicker of hope. For healing to start, I need him to consent to come with us.

"Tommy, if you come with us, I promise you'll be safe. You don't know me, but if you touch my hand, I'll show you my heart, and you can decide. Sound like a plan?" I dig into my newfound power and use it to send him a mental hug filled with love and compassion.

Tommy looks at my hand for a long moment. I block out the guys yelling about needing to go. Men can get so bossy when they have their testosterone in a knot. Keeping my hand extended, I use my mind to show Tommy an older version of himself as a sex angel fighting for justice. I have no idea if something like that is even conceivable, but now's not the time to dwell on trivial details. Something within makes me certain we can make it happen, so I go with the feeling. As the story plays out in my mind, Tommy relaxes. Little by little, inch by inch, he moves toward the safety of my grasp.

Streaks of light arc between us as the tip of his index finger touches mine. I force myself to stay still, letting him probe my mind, letting him see that I mean him no harm. The moment I close my hand around his, intense burning pain sears through me. Images of the torture this child endured batter me as I make his pain mine. Blackness starts to block my sight. My guys scream at me to let go, but I clutch harder. I will not lose this child. Determination gives me enough strength to say four words as I look into Troy's petrified face. "Take care of Tommy."

Troy's strong arms gather us as consciousness slips away. "I've got you."

BLACK ROSE AND THE THREE PRINCES

Queen Hera, always a gracious protector of heroes, sent the dead angels to Bardo to regenerate. For two years, relative calm reigned while Black Rose grew into her adolescence. No longer able to fight his evil desires, her foster father raped her, almost smothering her as he covered her mouth to silence her cries.

Atroyel's bond with Black Rose was so strong that her desperate cries smote his heart, pitching him into a pit of unbearable pain. Queen Hera took pity on him and agreed to help him and his brothers find his beloved Black Rose. Unsure of Black Rose's location, Queen Hera allowed each of the princes to inhabit a vessel on one of the three realms capable of housing a Nephilim life force. Armed with limited powers and no idea of her identity, Cassiel and Tristan searched their assigned realms and returned empty handed. Atroyel was sent to Earth in mortal form. All memory of life in the Afterlife was blocked by Earth's magnetic pull. With uncharacteristic blind faith, he had no idea what he searched for, but he knew he'd know it when he found it.

23

CASSIEL

I'm not going to take abuse anymore. The thought ripped through me a hair before a tremendous blast of power erupts as Aleah casts a stunning spell. By the time I pivot, a large man is pinned to the far wall, cuffed and manacled with magic. Patrons scream and start to rush from the room, but I focus my attention as several large men push their way through the crowd. Tristan and Atroyel step up beside me. We open the angelic connection between us full bore. A tattoo glows on two of the men, signaling their glyph magic. We instantly erect a defensive shield leaving the men on one side and us with Aleah, the boy, and the manacled guy on the other.

Despite her limited ability to control her power, Aleah made one attempt to reason with the guy before losing patience. Her slightly elevated heart rate, an awareness that's been with me from the moment we met, signals her determination as she pulls a *Star Wars* move and calls forth a light dagger. The strength of her magic almost shatters the defense shield.

The boy screams, and pain burns through me like acid as I open a portal to the manor. Even our combined power won't withstand the intense waves coming from the glyph magic for long. We need to move Aleah to safety before it shatters or reinforcements arrive.

"We wait!" Aleah's telepathic command reverberates through me as she turns her attention to the caged boy, oblivious to the chaos erupting around us, as if we have all the time in the world.

"Pick him up." Either she doesn't hear my silent command, or she chooses to ignore it. She sticks her arm into the cage and waits for Tommy to trust her enough to take her hand. Meanwhile, more glyph magic pummels the defense shield.

Another burst of power blasts from her when the boy takes her hand. She pulls him into her arms and sustains a healing spell for several long seconds before slumping to the ground. "Take care of Tommy."

Atroyel gathers her and the boy in his arms. *"I've got you."* My brother puts aside his fear and the barrage of emotion assaulting him and becomes a study in calm and control. *"I've got you, beauty."*

I reopen the portal and snap it shut the moment we step into the manor's great room. Silently, Raphael steps toward Atroyel and takes stock. Aleah's arms remain locked around Tommy, protecting this street urchin from the world despite the risk to her life. Her command rings through my head. *Take care of Tommy.* I open my senses, ready to manage the boy's terror, but he's more curious than anything. Whatever Aleah did, it had removed his torment and given him peace.

Atroyel holds Aleah while Raphael runs his hands over her, not quite touching. Tommy watches him, eyes wide, saying nothing. After a moment, Raphael mutters an incantation. Aleah's arms relax. Raphael extricates Tommy from her and hands him to me. When Raphael looks back at Aleah, his expression is grave. He gestures toward a large sofa where Atroyel gently lowers her curled form.

"Tell me what happened," Raphael says.

"That fucker Syrael got to her again. But how?" The panic in Tristan's voice matches that deep within.

"Long story short," Atroyel says, "Tommy's abductor tried to stop Aleah from rescuing him, triggering her fight response. There was a tremendous surge of power when she pinned the man to the wall and another when she touched the child. Her blue-white grace wove around and between them, absorbing the red and black threads of dark magic rising from the boy. As she sucked the last of the evil ether, she froze."

As if on cue, Aleah moans but doesn't move. Atroyel sits and pulls her into his arms. Her moans stop, thank the gods. Each moan contains pain so deep it pounds at my hard heart. Raphael's frown deepens.

"It would appear our Domina cast several high-level spells that drained a vast amount of her essential energy. Dark sex matter or magic designed to force the abductor to perform evil and perverse sex acts possessed the child. Not only did she cast a healing spell, but she also pulled the dark magic from the child to herself and used the last of her reserves to entrap the evil. From what I can see, she's put a shell around it, but the dark magic is a living thing, fighting hard for release." Raphael shook his head. "She doesn't have enough power left to expel the dark matter, so she's going to have to find a way to release it before it maims or kills her. She needs to have sex with an equally powerful being to release such powerful magic." Raphael pauses and looks at each of us, but I'd swear his gaze lingers on me.

"In the interest of saving time, I'll be blunt. I understand there's been some tension between you, resulting in two of you rejecting Domina as your divine mate. That will make things harder. We'll need to find a way to heal her injuries and refuel her power," Raphael says.

"She's fighting hard, but she's tiring." Atroyel answers without hesitation. "The pain's getting the best of her. She needs an injection of ether and fast. Let me know what I'm dealing with. I'll do what it takes." Atroyel looks at Raphael.

Raphael places a hand on Atroyel's shoulder. "You can't do this alone, son. Domina has inhaled dark magic that I've only read about in the Old Religion scrolls. Only the most powerful can destroy dark magic and only at great personal peril."

Atroyel stops his descent into despair mid-flight, squares his shoulders and reaches for the light. His determination and courage hit me like a physical blow. Atroyel has locked on saving his beloved, and nothing will deter him. Atroyel looks at Tristan as if examining an insect, and I barely recognize my brother. "Are you going to help me? Help her?"

Tristan opens his mouth, but Raphael cuts in. "To help her, you will need to open your connection with her." We each get another look. "Completely."

"In other words, can you put your selfish and self-serving feelings aside to save... Fuck, I'm sorry." Atroyel hugs Aleah closer and rotates his head, wrestling back his control. "I need your help. *We* need your help. This isn't personal. It's her life at stake."

Except it is personal, deadly personal. And he's asking more than I can give. If I open my essence to Aleah, this Nephilim will claim me. She's found a way to manipulate an angelic mating bond. That's the only explanation for the power she holds over us. I go through my list, reminding myself to remain resolute: she's nothing but trouble, she's a bossy and conniving bitch, she'll take over and ruin everything if I let her in.

"Perhaps Cassiel can read your Double Diary. The magic woven into your words will boost your sexual power." Raphael's words save my ass as I was one breath away from blowing the crevice between my brother and me into a yawning canyon.

I give a curt nod. "I can do that."

All eyes turn to Tristan, who looks as tormented as I've ever seen him. "I'm willing to do this on one condition," he says. Atroyel's impatience hits us like a slap. Tristan grimaces and continues. "I need a guarantee that we can reverse any of Aleah's magic I absorb. I'm with Cass on this one. There's something fishy about the mating bond." He rubs his brand.

"Druids don't have the power to manipulate dark magic," Raphael says. "Our magic is limited to control over natural elements and is ineffective in tampering with cosmic forces. We—" He stops abruptly and looks across the room. Atroyel cocks his head as if he hears something as well. After a few moments of what looks like a telepathic conversation, Raphael turns back to Tristan.

"Lady B gives her word that the gods will reverse any magic forced on you by the Chosen One. She also says, and I quote, to get on with it, for fuck's sake. Can't you see the woman's in agony?" Raphael and Atroyel exchange a glance, and I'd swear Atroyel can see the ghost. Things are changing too fast.

"I'm with your Lady B on this one," Atroyel says. "Tristan, are you with me or no?"

Tristan gives a reluctant nod.

"Any parting advice? This kind of magic is new to me," Atroyel admits. "Can the manor help us?"

"Keep her restrained until the lust wears off. You'll be able to tell," Raphael says. "I've prepared a room for you. The manor will keep the dark magic confined within the safe room. I'll release her from the holding spell when we're safely inside." He moves toward the door, and we follow our new Pied Piper.

24

TRISTAN

Fuck! Fuck! Fuck! Since punching a wall isn't a viable option, I opt for a stream of mental curses. What the fuck is wrong with me? One minute, I'm letting the romantic notion of a fated angelic mating bond reduce my gods-given cognitive functioning, and the next, I'm pining for something I can't have. For a brief moment, the universe lets me think I've found the true and enduring love I crave—someone who loves my mind, not my body. But Cass and Ali herself helped me see the hard truth. I was a fool for thinking she'd see past the cover and want to read the book.

Just when I turn my back on those cruelly false cupid moments, the universe plays another rotten trick by forcing me to heal this woman who's hurt me so badly. Usually, I could share and offload some of my emotional pain with Troy, but not this time. Troy has zero tolerance for any talk of Ali that even hints of disparagement. That's enough in itself, but I'm well aware of just how superficial I sound when I talk about the burden of my beauty and the reaction I'll get if I open the discussion. I've learned from experience that people have very little empathy for "beautiful people" problems. Maybe everyone is right, and it's time I accept reality—maybe my only worth is my looks. My beauty traps me.

I've tried talking to Cass, but, as expected, he leaped on the chance to say, "I told you so." For some reason not even known to him, Ali threatens Cass. He says she's got a carefully guarded secret he couldn't reach, and he has much stronger telepathic perception skills than I do. And now, my sounding board isn't an option.

It's with some trepidation that I follow Raphael into a room I haven't seen before. The walls are covered with heavy hunter green upholstery. Only the rich design keeps it from being labeled a padded cell, that and the size. We walk across a large room that, at first glance, could be a luxury gym with equipment lining the walls. A closer look reveals the equipment is every kind of BDSM furniture imaginable.

Troy gently places Ali's inert form on an oversized black leather couch tucked into a corner. Cass murmurs something to Tommy and seats him beside her then joins Raphael, Troy, and me in the center of the room.

"I'm worried about Tommy," Troy says. "He needs care and shouldn't be left alone. Aleah will want to see him when she's…" Troy's voice trails off. What the fuck do we call the state Ali's in? Possessed?

"When we are done here, I will take the boy to the Harmony Hills Treatment Centre for sexually abused children. The staff there are well equipped to take care of the boy until Domina can make other arrangements," Raphael says.

Troy nods, satisfied as he ticks another problem off the list in his mind. "What do we need to know?" Troy asks.

"Think of Blackstone Manor as a temple. We are standing in the ceremonial chamber used to contain and expunge dark magic," Raphael says. The dude could have been snatched out of the mortal's 1920s with his formal speech patterns.

"We rarely encountered a dark magic infestation. The grounds take care of most threats before they can get near the manor, but we're confident this room will contain the magic and stop Domina from harming herself. However, the manor will only intervene if she is in mortal danger, so it's up to you to keep her safe from less extensive damage."

"How the fuck do we do that?" Cass barks despite his only duty being one of reading.

Raphael ignores the rudeness. He pulls on a cord, and an elaborate harness anchored to the ceiling drops between us. "We have no idea how Domina will react to the dark matter. As the Chosen One, her divine light seems strong enough to contain it; however, we have no idea for how long. She is in pain, and the sex magic will force her into having sex to the point of self-harm."

"Her body will try to reject the dark magic." Troy's tone is so sure that we look at him in surprise. How the fuck can he know that? I can't even predict how she'll react, and I'm the one with the empathic gift. "I know my wife. I've had twenty years of seeing how her body reacts to foreign matter. She'll keep getting worse until she figures out a way to get rid of it."

"Then, my best advice is to undress and restrain her until you know what you are dealing with. Lady B believes with Atroyel's divine love and Tristan's healing magic, Domina has enough power to contain the dark matter if it escapes her body, but we have no means to destroy it."

"Anything else?" Troy starts removing his leather jacket. Cass is uncharacteristically quiet.

"As I said, once I leave, I'll seal the door and activate the containment spell. The manor will release the door when all traces of the dark matter are contained." Raphael points to a recessed cupboard. "You will find everything you need in the way of food and drink in the bar."

By this time, Troy is removing his shirt. Raphael gives him a quick nod. "Lady B also believes the dark matter will give Domina great strength, like a human on PCP. She will be consumed with lust when you release the spell and need to release sexual energy. What she can't release will attack her internal organs." Raphael gives us a penetrating look. "I expect tonight will put your stamina to the test."

He points to a side table beside the couch. "Your diaries are there. They contain powerful magic." This time Raphael gives Cass the look. "You will want to use them."

With a quick bow of his head he says, "When you are ready, say *'saor an spiorad'* to release the locking spell that will seal the room after I leave."

I repeat the words to release the spell in my head. It had sounded like *sir an spear-id*. Yes, I can remember that.

Raphael makes a sweeping gesture around the room. "If that will be all, I bid you all a good night."

I fully expect him to back his impeccably dressed body out through the door, but he lifts Tommy into his arms and walks out with his usual dignity.

Troy strips the rest of his clothes and tosses them over a chair. His focus is on one thing and one thing only—saving Ali. He strides over to her, sits beside her, and runs his hand over her back. "I've got you, beauty. We'll get through this together." The tenderness and determination in his voice pokes at the shield I've erected around my heart. Was this woman really devious and powerful enough to fool Troy's supernatural perception? Troy sets to work on removing Ali's clothing while I divest myself of mine at a much slower pace. Part of me yearns to be balls deep in Ali's hot cunt, but my thinking brain advises me to prepare to meet my doom.

"I could use a hand here." Troy's voice is clipped as he

struggles with Ali's jumpsuit. Cass, who has been remarkably silent, rises. I undress with reluctance, not sure if my rapid pulse is indicative of dread or desire. After they've stripped Ali naked, Troy carries her to the harness, where they secure the padding protecting her pelvis and ribcage before fastening her wrists, thighs, upper arms and ankles with suspension restraints.

Once Troy's assured himself that Ali's safely secured to avoid suspension trauma, he uses a remote to lift her body off the ground. The thick padding on the critical areas reduced the risk, but we'll need to change her position frequently and keep a close eye on her.

After placing Ali in a semi-seated position, Troy passes the remote to Cass. "Adjust her position every ten minutes or as needed," he says. Cass gives a curt nod. Due to the risk of suspension trauma, we have to be extra cautions. We all know the drill for keeping sex safe. After taking a long drink of water, Troy stands beside me. "You ready for this? Ready to drop your defenses?"

I'm ready, just not happy about being vulnerable to Ali's manipulative magic, but right now I have no choice. I nod.

Troy gives Ali another long look then glances at Cass. "Start reading."

Aleah @ October 1 @ 7:35 a.m.

My dearest Troy,

Just a quick note to let you know how very much I enjoyed watching you and being fucked by you last night. I loved spreading my legs and masturbating for you with your fingers rammed up my cunt. I bet your prissy little wife doesn't do that for you. Does she bend over on command

and let you ram your fingers up her cunt like you did to me yesterday? Does she immediately suck your cock on command with her hands held behind her back like I did yesterday? Will she do anything that you ask as I will?

I know, talking about your wife is taboo, but aren't taboos to be flaunted just a bit? I want you to put things in perspective—she may own you in every other way, but I am yours to command in all things sexual, which will, in turn, make you mine.

Of course, I may not always be in the mood to submit; we shall see. What will you do if I disobey? What kind of master will you be?

I won't ask much, but I will have a demand from time to time. Here's my first one: I particularly enjoyed watching you get into rubbing your cock and displaying yourself for me. Sometime soon, I want you to bring me off, then bring yourself off so that I can watch you come (and a little more light, please, so that I can see you 😊). I'm getting wet right now as I think of it.

I look forward to our evening at the Inn when you'll be all mine. No wife… Just you and me.

Your mistress,

Aleah the Great

2 5

ATROYEL

If someone had told me I'd willingly embrace intense pain to save another, I'd have asked if they'd lost their godsdamned mind. But that was before my death, and this is after. Because during the dying process, I opened my eyes and finally understood the tremendous personal cost Aleah'd paid on my behalf. As the disease consumed me, she marched down the road ahead of me, fully armed, clearing away debris and smoothing the path as much as possible. She was my *Brienne of Tarth* from *Game of Thrones*, my fiercest protector and advocate. But most of all, Aleah's unconditional and bottomless love set me free.

During one tough time, she sobbed because she couldn't shoulder the pain for me. The pain had made me more than a little irritable, and I'd called her stupid for even thinking such a thing. "Why would you put yourself in harm's way?"

The love coming from her as she responded had almost torn me apart. "You can call me whatever you like, babe. I'd do it because I love you, and I've had more practice with pain. Watching you in pain tears me apart. Bearing pain is easier."

Now, I understand what she meant. There isn't anything I wouldn't do for this woman, including die. This time, neither of us is in mortal danger, but Aleah has a major battle ahead of her to avoid being possessed by the dark magic. Time to get on with it. As Cass reads, Aleah's blue-white Nephilim grace mists over her skin, signaling the diary's word magic at work. I lean close to her ear and murmur, *"saor an spiorad."*

Ali sucks in a breath, and her eyes fly open. I don't need my connection with her to see her fear and pain—it leaks from every pore. She whimpers and tries to curl into the fetal position again. Her breathing is shallow and rapid, and her hands are closed fists. She twists her head from side to side before returning a frantic gaze to mine, and she tenses. "Where's Tommy?" Her tone is throaty, and she struggles to get the words out.

"He's safe. Raphael's got him," I say.

Her body sags back in the harness. "You've got to get out of here." Her voice is low as she enunciates each word carefully. Her determination and will flood through our mating bond, and for the first time ever, I feel the hum of her divine power. It's as if I've stepped close to a solar flare. She grits her teeth. "It's evil." She pants. "Can't let it free." More panting. "Says sex will free him. Can't let him hurt you."

Yet sex is what she needs to save her. She writhes, and desperation pours through our mating brand, igniting the divine light of our love. Cupping her cheeks in my palms, I force her to look at me.

"He can't hurt me. Your restraints and our magic will keep us safe." I have no idea if this is true, but I need her shields down. "Trust me. If Tristan and I focus on your healing, can you hold the cocoon you've put around the dark magic?"

When she nods, I step between her open legs. Her struggles increase as I spread her wet pussy lips and focus on the beauty the universe blessed me with. The scent of her lust is strong and heady, giving me an instant hard-on.

"Not one more fucking word, beauty. We're in this together." I push divine light through our brand as I plunge into her, balls deep. The instant we connect, her pain and terror punch me in the solar plexus. My angelic ability to withstand great pain gives me little protection against this evil magic. The dark ether making Aleah crave sex like a junkie needing a fix taints me. Every fucking neuron in my brain wants to bolt, go and hide, licking my wounds until it's safe to come out.

But that was the old Troy, the Troy who often took the easy road to avoid any discomfort. The Troy who'd been happy to let Aleah protect him from most of life's unpleasantness. Agony and raw lust blaze through me with each thrust. But I will be here for my beauty. I let the dark aphrodisiac fuel my libido while I try to absorb the pain.

Help me. Please. I'm not sure whether the mental scream comes from Aleah or me, but it works. My pain eases as Tristan's divine power transfers through our triplet bond.

"Steady. Focus on the words. On the love." Tristan's voice soothes as he redirects my attention.

Once again, my brother's wisdom steadies me. I open myself and let the magic from our words of love seep into me as Cass reads. The words remind me of all the roles Aleah has played in my life—mistress, wife, lover, friend, sex slave, companion, caregiver, and so many more. Some passages are like a punch to the gut... still.

You are my mistress. Yes, in so many ways, so much more and better than my wife. As my mistress, you certainly have the freedom attributed to this status. Yes, I love you, but you do have the freedom to decide if you wish to remain my mistress. If so, never forget that it is on my terms because I want it that way, and you want and need it that way.

As I embrace the erotic muscle memories from those happy days, the remaining pain sensations change to fuel for the lust burning through me. I do what I hadn't done enough of in our first lifetime together, I trust in our love and channel it through our mating bond.

"Your love gives me strength!"

Her love, in turn, gives me strength, and I renew my efforts to bring us both to the orgasm that will release her simmering power. I let her words guide my actions.

I'm thinking of how you run your hands up and down my body. I'm feeling your lips sucking my nipples. I'm smelling your scent as it changes in your excitement. I'm hearing your low moan when you can't hold it back anymore—this I especially love.

Tristan kisses Aleah, and his hand snakes into the wet well between her spread legs. She moans and deepens the kiss, sucking his essence, as he uses her glistening dew to paint circles around her nipples. Aleah thrashes until his hand returns to her clit. I fight the pulses of pain as the dark magic fights to free itself. Tristan's eyes lock with mine. He feels it too. We strengthen the bond between us. We have one focus and one only—save Aleah.

Cass continues reading Troy's words.

You're patient, loving, considerate, compassionate, empathetic, sensitive, caring, dedicated, organized, ambitious, independent, trusting, trustworthy, honest, giving, open, friendly, challenging, reliable, assertive, knowledgeable, thoughtful, flexible, understanding—to name a few! I fell in love with your mind as you are very, very smart!
OK, OK… The truth is I fell in love with you because you're hot and fuck like crazy!

The truth and love in those words I'd written that day so long ago blazes through our bond, and divine energy flares between us. I grab one of Aleah's hips to brace us and slam into her. On cue, Tristan increases the rhythm on her clit. Aleah's solar flare explodes into divine light as our orgasms hit, and I'm not sure if the power comes from her or me.

Power and white light burst from Aleah, and for several heart-stopping beats, there's absolute stillness. Then Aleah's eyes spring open, and my semi-erect cock slides out.

"Sit me up." Her command is urgent, and Cass uses the remote to adjust her position. Her wrists are bound and her arms outstretched. She stares at her left hand and starts whispering.

"I want you out of me, so here's what's going to happen. You're going to stop giving me grief and come out here where I can see you." Her voice gains strength as her confidence grows. My eyes rivet on her hand. Energy whirls over her fingers, moving faster than my enhanced eyesight can follow. When it slows, a large translucent white sphere floats above Aleah's palm, with thousands of red and black ether strands twisting inside it.

"Got you." Aleah's voice is weak but triumphant.

"Now, what are you going to do with it?" Cass joins us, staring at the globe in amazement.

Aleah gives that mischievous little smile I love. "I have no fucking idea, but I can't think about it right now. I'm too weak." She gives the sphere another hard look. "You're going to be a good bad-boy and go wait over there until I can figure out what to do with you." She issues the command with confidence and assurance as if she's been ordering around magic her entire life.

The sphere glides toward the skylight high above us. "And no peeking."

The energy shifts in the room, and a dense box captures the globe. The manor protects the Chosen One.

Aleah sags in the harness as her energy wanes, but she manages a wicked grin at Tristan and me in turn. "And now, boys, I need sex and plenty of it. You two promised me a threesome." She leans back and closes her eyes. "Oh, and Cass, keep reading. You've got the best bedroom voice."

ALEAH

There's no doubt about it. That shit coming out of me is magic and that blows any remaining doubt dragons in that area to smithereens. I have fucking superpowers. Look out, Wonder Woman. She may have the lasso of truth, but I have light blasts and light daggers. I can't wait to find out just how powerful I am and reflect on the responsibility that comes with it, but right now, I need sex. Badly. And that need is consuming my ability to do anything else.

Traces of the dark magic still slither through me. Since I can't seem to get rid of it, I will have to ride with it. "You two promised me a threesome."

After my pronouncement, all three guys stare at me in varying degrees of horror. Although I can feel each of them to differing extents through this new connection linking them to me, their feelings flash across their respective faces. Cass and Tristan are at war with their feelings in a way that's far too high maintenance for me at the moment. Troy wonders where he'll find the wherewithal for another session if it's going to be anything like the last. When the gods joined us in this angelic mating bond, my heart divided into four pieces. His essence took up residence in one of the four chambers of my heart. He's nestled there, part of me, and he's having a teeny tiny bit of performance anxiety. Now that's something in the sex department I know how to handle. At least with Troy.

It had taken a while, given most of my sex ed came from trashy romance novels and sketchy sex manuals. When in doubt, do research, so when Troy had seemed a wee bit touchy in the performance department, I tried the best advice I could find. I'd named his cock and talked about what a "big boy" he was. The result? Mild amusement but not the boost juice I'd been hoping for. Nope, what works with Troy is lots and lots of foreplay… and promises of a blow job.

I'm sore as hell from the thrusting workout Troy just gave my lady bits, and every nerve ending in my body screams from the pain from the dark magic, yet all I can think about is getting banged… and the many exciting ways that can happen. Images of all kinds of activities flash through my mind—flogging, spanking, nipple clamps, e-stim play, and fire play, to name a few. Things I once loathed now suddenly seem appealing.

While Troy stalks off to grab a drink of water, Tristan fusses with my restraints, and my attention rivets on him. Although faint, his essence resides in the third quarter of my newly formed heart, but my intuition is on overdrive despite the pain.

Tread carefully with this one. I swear Nye's voice drifts through my head. Tristan wants me and needs me.

His yearning is almost overwhelming at the moment… and so is the shadow of rejection.

The thought of rejection brings a flood of shame messages as my doubt dragons leap at the chance to take over. *That's right, shame him. Show him how it feels to be rejected. Put on your best snark and ask him how he feels about you forcing yourself on him.* The nasty messages pick up speed until I slam the brakes on.

I need Tristan too. And it's not just about the sex the dark magic makes me crave; his place in my heart tells me otherwise. But he doesn't seem to know that, and I have no fucking idea how to convince him. There's so much we need to learn about each other, but he gets me on a whole different level than Troy does. Where Troy steps back and pulls me with him to observe life, Tristan jumps into the pool and prances around with me. I crave the slow, sweet smile that lights his face when he sees me, the laser focus that makes me the center of his universe. So I stare into those gorgeous blue eyes smoky with longing and will the universe to guide me. Because I don't want to think right now. I want to feel.

"You need a drink." Tristan leans away from his discomfort by rushing off and returning with a glass and a straw. Gently cupping the back of my head, he brings the straw to my mouth and watches intently as I take several long hauls. The water joins the double diary words feeding me low intensity energy pulses, but I'm weak and have no reserves against Tristan's exposed essence. It seems he has to open his connection to me to heal me and has no protection from the hurt I've somehow caused him.

I wish my hands were free so I could touch him. Instead, I let my desire flow through our connection. *I want to know you, body and soul.* He ignores my silent entreaty while he gets rid of the water glass.

Tristan wrestles with his pain and lands on being macho man as his savior. He channels Thor—I flash on Chris Hemsworth—or Superman... *Oh, Henry Cavill...* Not at all the kind of thoughts I should be having at a serious moment like this, so I decide to blame my new superpowers for my wayward thoughts. That makes no sense at all, but I'd stopped worrying about making sense the day I was "diagnosed" a menopausal woman to explain a myriad of symptoms. I'm happy to add a raging libido to my rapidly growing list.

Tristan flexes his impressive biceps in a very Achilles-in-*Troy* way, bringing me back to this alternate reality. I lick my lips as I ponder when I started liking ripped muscles. My gaze drifts downwards. Okay, I almost get whiplash as I fasten onto one particular ripped muscle making its presence known between his legs. I usually gravitate toward the lean, athletic type, but all kinds of new sexy feelings are coursing through me right now as I take in Tristan's muscular frame.

"I want you too, babe." Yup, he flexes that muscle too. "My turn."

I watch him pad toward me. When he's close enough to touch me, he runs his hands over my body, assessing. His light touch acts like an accelerant on my libido, and I ache to have him inside me as my body responds in its usual wacky way. Troy and I learned early that my clitoral orgasms acted like a fuse blowing open the receptors in my G-spot and other erogenous zones. When Tristan's finished his assessment, he gives a nod of satisfaction and makes a show of hefting his junk for me.

I lick my lips. I can't help it. I still can't get over just how big Tristan is. My body craves his healing essence, and I crave his body. He teases me for several long agonizing moments by sliding his fingers through my hot folds and using my juices to lube his thick shaft. My body almost convulses as he places a hand on my shoulder to anchor me before entering me. His balls slap against my ass cheeks as my vagina stretches around his girth, and he lets out a low moan.

Sexual electricity sears through me, burning away all rational thought. My pussy answers Tristan's throbbing cock with a few pulses of her own. Having him seated deep within feels right as if he were made for me. I close my eyes so I can focus on Tristan's touch. Cass's voice resumes reading our double diary, keeping a steady stream of Troy's and my love percolating in the background.

"Oh no, you don't." Tristan's low growl makes my eyes snap wide open, switching my focus from the inferno between my legs to his intense gaze. For the first time, I see his genetic similarity to Troy. The same need for connection blazes in his eyes. His essence is open to me, so I know he doesn't want to expose himself this way, but he's tenacious and persevering, and like me, he'll always err on the side of doing the right thing.

"You will look at me. You *will* know it's me you're fucking." Tristan's command laces through me, and I'm not sure if it's magic or our connection that takes hold. Suddenly, though, I can't do anything but look at him, and oh yes, dear God, I know this is Tristan. I need it to be Tristan. Not Troy. Not Brad Pitt. Tristan.

I look deep into his eyes and let him see that place in my heart housing the tiny part of our connection he wasn't able to pull back. *"I need you... body, mind, and soul."*

"No talking." His command tells me that even my thoughts scream too loudly for him, so I'll have to let my body do the talking just like I'd had to do with Troy all those years ago.

I meet his eyes and telegraph my desire for him and him alone. And I let his healing essence soothe some of the dark lust raging through me. As his cock starts a long slow dance with my G-spot, I show him how his fucking is like sipping the smoky-sweet-spice of Mezcal, giving me similar feelings of euphoria and joy.

The restriction of the restraints forces me to use my small muscles to punctuate our empathic conversation. In reality, it's more of a debate because Tristan's lust can't hide his exposed hurt and rejection. But he's met his match. When it comes to finding ways to share feelings with my body, I'm the queen of debate. As each thrust moves me closer to another powerful orgasm, I parry with a message of my own. *"You can run, but you can't hide, Tristan. You're part of me now."*

CASSIEL

I've found a quiet spot in the house where I can have a drink of Mezcal and get my shit together before Aleah's command performance dinner. Someplace where no one's going to try to read my thoughts or manipulate my feelings. Someplace where there's no Aleah.

If she could just be a piece of ass, that would be one thing. Aleah's a fuckfest delight, there's no doubt about it, and I'd like nothing better than to tame that tiger. Like Atroyel, she reminds me of a big cat, although the more I think about it, she's the one who does the hunting and gathering in their relationship… more of a lioness leading her pride. Much like a lion pride, Atroyel and Aleah work as a symbiotic unit.

If I admit the truth to myself, I see another side to my brother. Before Aleah, Atroyel rarely stuck his neck out, preferring to stay far under the radar and observe. But now he's like a fucking lion, doing sweet fuck all until there's a threat to his pride, pun intended. He hated being out of control, so he had learned to reign in his explosive temper at an early age. As a result, he rarely put himself into a situation he couldn't control. But when Atroyel leaps into action, look out. I've only seen his violent side once or twice in battle, but that was enough. His dark side only reared its head when there was an imminent threat to Tristan or my life and when Atroyel had no time to think before acting. But there's something very different about him now. Our link is getting stronger every day we're together again, showing there's a new stubborn strength to him now. A strength that's fueled by Aleah's love.

Parts of their diary have blasted past the armor surrounding my hard heart. I have to admit there's something authentic and enviable between my brother and her. For some reason, when he said things like "I fell in love with your mind as you are very, very smart!" and "The truth is I fell in love with you because you're hot and fuck like crazy," the sense of longing that came over me damn near drove me to my knees. And I don't go down on my knees for anyone. But her love comes at a cost, and Atroyel's traded his freedom for the old ball and chain.

I flash back to the night before last when I'd had to endure the torture of watching and not fucking the most sensual woman I've ever shared a scene with. That's saying a lot, given the Fae have made fucking their life's work. Atroyel had grumbled that he'd been born into the wrong species; that is, until he joined with Aleah. That night when I'd had her had been the best sex of my life… and then I'd gone and fucked it all up.

Even sex angel lords need post-coital recovery time, and last night, I'd broken down and spelled the guys in a way that allowed me to keep my distance after they'd put in hours of full-tilt fucking. Whether it was the magic or natural proclivity driving her, she'd reveled in having two men fuck her, one right after the other. It had been bad enough being in the same room with them without participating, but I'd had to listen to her sounds. Like the slight intake of breath she takes just before her orgasm erupts. That tiny sound grabbed me by the balls and held on.

Once the raging inferno left by the black ether had simmered, I'd spelled the guys by flogging Aleah, who I secured on the St. Andrew's Cross. I refused to admit how much I wanted to know how she'd respond to some decent impact play. Aleah had been abundantly clear about her intolerance for pain, but her responses hinted at a desire, or perhaps just a curiosity for sensation play. Since she was already highly sexually charged, I decided to give her a Florentine flogging using two thin floggers to start. Her tight ass twitched as I slowly drew the long tails across her body to prepare her for the flogging. After drawing out the antici-pation, I backed up to arm's length and braced myself as I examined Aleah's flawless back.

With one flogger in each hand, I started an overlapping pattern of light strikes at the top of her back and worked my way down, careful to avoid the no-go zones of the neck, kidneys, tailbone, spine, and hips. Aleah was exceptionally responsive when I hit her ass and thighs, so I focused my attention there when I switched to a single flogger with thicker tails.

Aleah's ability to orgasm seemed limitless, and I was curious to explore. From a purely research point of view... or that's what I told myself.

But I'd refused to penetrate her. Refused to do anything that would strengthen the bond between us. By this time, the facts are so clear even I can't deny them. I'm intended to be one of Aleah's fated mates. I'm not happy; I'd die before I let some woman take over my life. Not this lad. I have no problem with the status quo, none at all. The three of us had managed quite nicely on our own for a thousand years. If Atroyel wants to give up peace of mind for a piece of tail, then best of luck to him. Tristan and I will be just fine on our own.

Keep telling yourself that, fuckwad.

But now the fucking woman's found a way to trap me. The child Tommy… and just how magnificent Aleah had been when she'd saved him. She didn't know about my weakness for abused children. She couldn't. My brothers are the only living souls that know my secret, and they'd never tell anyone. This vulnerability is my Achilles heel. Aleah acted with compassion and empathy. She'd been a warrior. There's no other way to describe her. Despite having no awareness of what it's like to work with magic, she didn't hesitate. There was little I could fault in her strategic thinking, either. Except, I would have killed the bastard. No second chances. I start to get hard as I picture her, arms outstretched, divine light and grace pouring from her and then kick the image to the curb. Hard.

Aleah is trouble, whether she intends to be or not. I let the alcohol punctuate my decision, with its deceptive euphoric glow, and convince myself of the righteousness of my anger. Convincing myself I'm not drowning in fear and desire. After all, I don't have enough time for a cold shower, and I need to steel myself for our confrontation about Tommy's care. Raphael delivered the boy to the Harmony Hills Treatment Center. I checked on the boy yesterday and today, and the center is the perfect place for him to recover. I do not doubt that Aleah will rave about adopting the boy or some such nonsense, but he needs professional care that she can't deliver.

I try to make Tommy the problem, but I've never been one to lie to myself. My inability to identify just what's troubling me makes me want to punch something. Unlike my brothers, I have no problem with violence and thrive on my reputation as a ruthless and dangerous foe. Something threatened our family unit, but I'll be damned if I know exactly what. And I'm getting nothing insightful through the link with my brothers. Atroyel continues to swim in a tank of mating bond bliss while Tristan's slipped into one of his mindless states. My intuition tells me that all roads point to Aleah.

With a long sigh, I finish my drink and head to the dining room. Tristan falls in step with me as I navigate my way through the halls. Since our trip to the Acquired Taste sex club, he's stuck close to me for moral support. Unfortunately, he can't block the hurt and confusion caused by… bleeding through our link despite his attempts otherwise. I resist the urge to squeeze his shoulder in empathy. He'll get over it.

There's no one in the dining room, despite the formally set table. We follow the voices to the kitchen, where we find Atroyel and Aleah perched at the large island chatting with Raphael.

My heart almost stutters to a halt as my eyes light on her. I stop at the built-in bar between the kitchen and dining room and pour myself another Mezcal while I get a grip on my traitorous feelings. Because there's no fucking reason my cock should have bolted upright at the sight of her in the loose-fitting asymmetrical black top and coordinating pants. The damned outfit hides every curve on her petite frame and should look like a sack, but instead, it teases my cock with hints of small, firm breasts and ass cheeks begging to be spanked. Tristan exhales a slow whistle as his excitement transmits through our triplet link. Some thread deep inside me starts to rise like a vine reaching for sunlight. I snap the sunroof shut before the roots take hold. Or so I tell myself as I gulp a fortifying mouthful of the Mezcal and let the delicious smell of roasting meat pull me into the kitchen.

"Bob may have a point," Atroyel says with a laugh.

"Although I would have said getting fucked is the only time your brain disengages."

A huge grin transforms Aleah's face. "That's a supposition. We need more data before we can leap to conclusions like that." She gives a little wave in our direction, but both she and Atroyel gaze toward the ceiling. Finally, after a momentary pause, Atroyel barks out a laugh.

"That may be your experience, but stamina is my middle name. Game on." My brother displays new quiet confidence as he makes this announcement to thin air. Atroyel never plays games and is not a betting man.

"You heard her. Can you see her too?" Aleah's face is alive with delight.

"I can hear her. What are we playing?" Tristan asks. "I'm in."

TRISTAN

"What are we playing? I'm in." Those words exit my mouth before I have time to think and remember that I'm going to let my brain rule my emotions for once in my life. Something about this woman speaks to my heart before my good sense has a chance to take over.

Ali and Troy turn toward me as I speak. Each appears startled. "You can hear her too?" Ali asks.

"Hear who? Who the fuck are we talking about?" Cass hates to be in the dark.

"We're talking about Nye, our hostess," Troy says. "She's—
"

"I know who she is." Cass's clipped tone cuts Troy off. "Why are we talking about the Druid high priestess?"

"It would appear that as Domina comes into her power, she can share her vision of Lady B through her mating bond," Raphael says.

"I can hear but can't see her," I say.

"Seems to be working because I can see and hear her," Troy says. "It's good to see you again, Nye." He drops his gaze to Ali and touches her cheek briefly with the backs of his fingers. She rewards him with a soft, sweet smile that makes me ache with longing.

"Look at you getting all romantic on us, Atroyel. You're looking a lot better than the last time I saw you." A distinctive Welsh lilt, which I assume belongs to Anais, the Druid high priestess, fills the room. Nye's disembodied voice brims with approval. Troy has a knack for finding favor with older women. I can't see her, but the sound of her voice brings back the memory of our meeting. Nye and Queen Hera had made it quite clear that accepting the mission to help Ali take down Lord Syrael wasn't a choice.

"It's all on account of my beauty here." Troy's voice echoes the peace and joy humming through our triplet link.

For a brief moment, I'm envious until I remember my new resolve—do what needs to be done to defeat Lord Syrael, then Cass and I will go about our business. I ignore the painful throbbing in my deltoid as I block the circuit connecting me with Troy and focus on Cass's misery. Our older brother's hurting because he thinks he's losing what remains of our family, and one of us needs to be there for him. As usual, by default, picking up the pieces after Troy's meltdowns falls to me.

While Ali and Troy continue to gaze at each other adoringly, Raphael plates appetizers, decants a bottle of red wine and then looks at Ali. "Would Domina prefer to dine in the kitchen or dining room?"

"Here is good, thanks, Raphael." Ali picks up her wine glass and takes a seat at the round table. Troy takes the seat to her right, leaving three empty seats. Cass frowns but says nothing as he takes the seat beside Troy. Desperate to keep distance between Ali and me, I take the seat beside Cass.

"I assume you'll be joining us, Raphael?" Troy pushes his sleeves over tanned forearms, acting as if he's lord of the manor. Although he's blocked our link to him, it's clear that he's decided about Ali, us, and our future.

"Yes, Master Troy, as soon as I've attended to your needs," the old caretaker says.

Ali pats the empty seat beside her as Raphael places several trays on the table. "That's good enough, Rafi. We're quite capable of helping ourselves. However, we need your brains, not your brawn right now, and I need to practice my magic."

"Yes, *Rafi*. Do have a seat and regale us with the wisdom of the ages." Nye's sarcasm rings out loud and clear.

Tonight, the butler's dressed impeccably in what looks to be a bespoke tailored gray suit made of a super-luxurious fabric. "As you wish, Domina." Raphael takes his seat without any recognition that he heard Nye's taunt.

Ali manages to keep a lid on her eagerness to get started. Despite the wall of detachment she's erected around her heart, her excitement seeps through the cracks into tiny hidden pockets within me as her gaze sweeps over me. Once we've all filled our plates, Ali sits back and raises her wine glass.

"Before we get started, I want to thank you all for helping me get through the other night." She raises the glass skyward then takes a long sip before setting the glass down. "I've had a lot of time to think while the black magic worked its way out of my system, and I want to brainstorm strategy with you. But first, fill me in on what's happening with Tommy, please?" Ali focuses the spotlight of her attention onto Cass.

"The boy is fine." Cass's detached voice has an uncharacteristic undercurrent of anger that nets a sharp glance from Troy and me. It isn't often that anything shows past his calm and observant demeanor. "I took care of him as you asked. You don't need to worry your pretty little head about him."

I don't need our connection to see the wash of heat that

rushes through Ali as the shells of her ears turn bright red. She takes a deep breath, extends her arms, palms down, and then pushes them toward the table.

"Babe, what are you doing?" Troy asks.

"I'm stopping the acid wash of shame." She says this as if it's a common occurrence.

"You aren't going to let that little shite get away with that patronizing attitude, are you?" Nye's voice sounds somewhere above my head.

Ali looks in the direction of the voice and gives a tight smile. "I'm not sure how I'm going to respond." She gives Cass a penetrating look. "For some reason, a lot of Cass's comments trigger a shame response in me, and I've got to figure out why before I know how to respond."

"Let me guess, more of your psychobabble." Acid drips from Cass's voice.

Ali gives him a fuck-you smile that doesn't reach her eyes. "Yes, exactly that. Bob reminded me that with my power comes great responsibility as I journey toward wholehearted living. So yes, psychobabble." Ali pops a stuffed mushroom into her mouth and chews thoughtfully.

"I'm with you, beauty. Show us the way," Troy says. He leans over and drops a kiss on Ali's plump lips.

Fuckwad. Cass's insult rings loud and clear through our brother bond, as does Troy's blatant refusal to engage. Another strand of hope tickles the weird new sensation in my chest, and the black rose tattoo on my shoulder pulses in response.

"I'm hoping all of you will show me the way; after all, you know how to use your power. And all of this is new to me. But we digress. Back to Tommy." Ali beams her spotlight back onto Cass, and steely determination rearranges her features. "Please elaborate on the meaning of fine and how you took care of him."

"I'd have thought someone as well versed in the use of words as you would know the definition of fine, but here goes." Cass's stern gaze punctuates the vitriol in his voice.

Simultaneously, anger, fear and resignation hit me through the psychic switchboard that's been happening since we met Ali, but I can't identify the source. The anger is most certainly from Cass, and I'd wager the acceptance of the inevitable comes from Troy. That left the fear. Was it coming from Ali? If so, why? What did she have to be afraid of? She straightened in the chair, looked at Troy and gave her head a quick shake.

Troy's lips thin as he focuses on Cass. His flash of anger rises to meet Cass's punch in a boxing match I'd refereed many times.

"You're being an asshole, Cassiel." The cold steel in Troy's voice makes me shiver. "Tread very carefully, brother, and understand me clearly." Troy leans forward and rests his forearms on the table. "Nothing and no one is going to come between Aleah and me ever again, and that includes you and the gods."

"You tell him." Nye's voice now comes from my far left.

"Then why are you still here?" Cass's equally cold tone asks.

Ali places a small hand on Troy's forearm. He covers it with his without taking his gaze from Cass. "You can thank this woman for that. For some reason I've never been able to fathom, family connection is hugely important to her. I'm ambivalent. As far as I'm concerned, she's all I need." He glances at her briefly and gives her hand another squeeze. "Once we're done with Syrael, we're out of here."

Troy and Cass have another glare down as their tempers clash. I brace myself; nothing good ever results when Cass challenges Troy. The fear coming through my link ramps up a notch, making it clear it's coming from Cass.

"Enough." Ali's voice cracks the tension like a whip. "No one's going anywhere at the moment." She gives Troy a brief appreciate-you smile. "Right now, we need to focus on our mission, and we need your help." She looks between Cass and me.

"Tomorrow, I go to work on figuring out what all of this Chosen stuff means," Ali says. "But first, I need to keep my promise to Tommy."

"You won't be allowed to see him. All new intakes spend seven days under observation without contact," Cass says. "I have a meeting with his doctor in the morning. I'll update you."

Ali studies him for a moment. "Fine. I'll go with you." Her tone leaves no room for argument. "When we get back, I need help. As wonderful and scary as it is to have these new powers, I have no frigging idea how to use them."

"We'll leave that to Atroyel the Magnificent," Cass spits out, "since he's the answer to all your prayers and— Ouch!" He leaps to his feet with his head twisted to the side and starts moving toward the door.

"We'll have no more of that, you big ninny," Nye's voice comes from Cass's side. "Maybe a wee time out will help you come to your senses."

But Cass can't hear Nye. So instead, he looks at Ali with enough fury to incinerate plutonium. "I'll get you for this." His voice is low and cold. Ali looks confused. Troy looks amused.

"Aleah isn't doing it." Troy's bark of humor washes through our brother bond as he leaps to the defense of his beloved.

"It's true," I hasten to add. "Nye's doing it."

"But—" Nye yanks Cass out of the room before he can say anything else.

I jump up and follow. "I'd better go with him."

"Maybe you should go too, babe. I don't want to come between you and your brothers." Ali's voice fills with worry.

"This is on Cass, beauty, and if they can't see that, fuck them." Troy's voice is firm and final. "Now, enough of them. It's our time now" His words fade as the distance grows between us but not before I get a blast of their shared love… love I can never have.

ALEAH

"Morning, beauty." Troy joins me in Nye's dressing room as I fuss at my clothes in front of a full-length mirror. Typically, it takes me about thirty seconds to decide what to wear after checking the weather forecast, but this morning brings an unusual level of contemplation. What is the perfect outfit for the Chosen? Something elegant but not flashy. Understated yet showing strength… but not too much, which nixed the power suit I'd started with. Thankfully, Nye's wardrobe gives me plenty of choices, and I flip through the hangers looking for understated elegance.

I smooth my hands over the black satin midi dress that's only embellished with two gold buttons on one shoulder and five more on the opposite side above a low thigh slit. Perfect choice. The flicker of desire that simmers through our mating bond takes a little leap. Troy drops a kiss on the top of my head. "You look good." Those three words are high praise coming from Troy, and I give him an appreciative smile. Troy isn't one for a lot of accolades, as he calls them, never was.

"Unless you need me, Tristan and I will stay here and see

what we can figure out for our best defense against Lord Syrael," Troy says.

"That makes sense." I smile up at him with my approval. Now that Troy has a mission, he'll march toward it with single-minded determination, eliminating all obstacles within his control. I'd learned long ago that the best thing to do when he's in one of these frantic modes is to stay out of his way. We'd spent hours last night talking about how best to approach this latest phase in our life journey.

In our individual ways, Troy and I explored every contingency we could think of before settling on needing more information to figure out the next steps in defeating Lord Syrael and worrying about the destined mate harem situation. Troy had also convinced me to put worrying about his relationship with his brothers on hold until we removed Syrael's threat. I agreed. I have more than enough to focus on figuring out my new identity and trying to save my life, but letting go of my worry about family isn't quite so easy.

"You ready?" Troy squeezes the back of my neck before he heads toward the door.

"Hold on a minute, babe. Are you sure about this? I don't want to be the one responsible for coming between you and your brothers." But, try as I might, I can't get rid of the dread that washes through me at the idea of being held responsible for breaking up another family.

Troy's human family had never warmed to me, although I'd been blind as a bat to their reaction because I wanted a family so badly. Troy's family could have been the model for one of the perfect family television shows. When he'd introduced me as part of the family, he'd been so matter of fact about their commitment to me that I'd assumed what he said was gospel. I'd been shocked and amazed when I found out that his siblings thought I was "difficult and different" and blamed me for standing between them and their beloved brother. The discovery had shattered me, and I'd realized that I was truly on my own. And here we are again.

Troy strides back to me and jabs his finger in the air for emphasis. "Are we going to do this again? We went through this last night. Many times. You are not breaking apart our family. You are my destined mate and the most important thing in my life. If my idiot brothers can't appreciate your beauty and strength, then fuck them. We have a plan, so let's get it done." This time, he leaves, and I take several quick steps to catch up with his long stride.

Raphael, Cass, and Tristan wait in the foyer. Nye is nowhere in sight. Cass and Raphael wear tailored three-piece suits in different shades of gray. Cass's white striped shirt has a rounded collar with a band that sports a single jewel instead of a button. He shoots his cuffs as he gives me an appreciative once-over. Then he catches his reaction and shuts it down. But it's too late because I've seen it. Despite my latest vow to remain unaffected where Cass and Tristan are concerned, heat bubbles in my lady bits. The man does know how to carry a suit.

Speaking of eye candy, Troy and Tristan look equally as GQ in a casual sort of way. Troy wears jeans and a beautiful navy knit sweater, while Tristan wears black jeans and a gray knit. Both sweaters accentuate their chiseled pecs and sleeves pushed up over defined forearms with the most delicious sprinkle of fine hairs decorating them. Gods, how I love being wrapped up in those arms. *Focus, Aleah.*

"Good morning," I say as I join the group.

"Good morning, Domina. I trust you slept well." Raphael hands me my bag, and I smile with my thanks.

"Here's how things will go," Cass says. Seemingly unaffected by social niceties or the clashes we've had before, he tries to strut his alpha-male stuff. I say nothing. One thing I learned about men long ago: when they decide to play the "little woman" game, ignore them entirely and do what I need to do. Before being chosen, I'd have been all in his face, challenging his authority over me. So instead, although this calling stuff is new to me, I decide to treat it like a new management position and observe the power structure. There's no need to tell him I'll do what *I* decide is best.

"When we arrive at Harmony Hills, we'll be meeting with the administrator, Katherine King, to review the results of Tommy's initial assessment. I'll take the lead. Once we've decided on next steps, I'll meet with Tommy while the staff gives you three a tour of the facilities," Cass says.

I nod, reminding myself that today's goal is to watch and learn—after I make sure Tommy will get the care he needs. As for Cass being the one to see him, we'd see about that. Cass makes a sweeping motion with his hand, and a portal opens up showing several buildings nestled on acres of forest, fields and meadowland. I control the urge to gush over how cool it is to be able to travel this way.

I point to the portal. "Will I be able to do that?" I direct my question to the group at large.

"Potentially," Raphael answers. "According to the Old Faith, the Chosen has the power of Supreme Voice, which means you have the power to create and command using your voice. What we need to help you discover is how strong your power is. Once you've finished with your business, we can get to work, Domina. As you command." He bows his head slightly in that charming way he has. Odd, but giving me the vibe that he's on my team. He uncorks a small vial and hands it to me. One whiff tells me it's the nasty nectar that hides me from Lord Syrael, I wrinkle my nose and down the god-awful stuff.

"Thanks, Rafi," I say. "I appreciate that." I drop a quick kiss on Troy's luscious lips, and he gives my butt cheek a quick squeeze. Promises for play when the work's put away.

I'm already leaning toward Tristan when I realize what I'm doing and give him an awkward little wave.

"See you later," I say to the room at large.

Cass frowns at Troy. "Aren't you coming?"

"It will be a better use of our time if Tristan and I stay here and learn more about what we're dealing with." Troy looks at Tristan, who's been remarkably quiet lately. "Okay by you?"

Tristan nods. Cass gives another frown and shakes his head. We step through the portal and walk up to the sprawling rustic ranch house. Cass opens the front door and leads us into a large foyer where a petite Black woman stands beside a large desk outside of double etched glass French doors. She strolls forward to meet us and extends her hand as she nears. My radar goes on instant alert as it always does when I'm in a new situation, only now it amplifies to space force. I wait for the usual wall of fear to hit me when I'm around people, but there's barely a trickle. Instead, love and trust from the surroundings blanket me. What a great atmosphere for a kid. Hell, if I wasn't at Blackstone Manor, I might take a retreat here myself.

"Welcome back, Cassiel. And you must be Aleah." She gives me a warm smile.

With a firm handshake then sandwiching my hand between hers, she says, "Welcome to Harmony Hills. Call me Kat. Tommy's very eager to see you, but first, let's get you some refreshments and talk. Would you prefer coffee or tea? We can also do expresso, latte, or cappuccino."

My intuition has always been very good, so I let my new spidey senses go on full alert. I've been in all kinds of institutional settings, but there's no sense of the usual clinical vibe. After a rapid inventory of our rustic and kid-friendly surroundings, I turn my attention to our hostess and see that she's bathed in light. Light that I can read. Kat's pure red aura radiates with fearless and unapologetic passion. Cool.

"I'll take a caramel latte, please," I say.

The young man behind the desk stands. "No problem. Any flavor shots?"

"Caramel, thanks," I say.

"Where are my manners?" Kat asks. "Meet my assistant, George."

I shoot George a quick smile because I'm too busy reading his aura to do more. Several different shades of orange mingle, telling me George's considerate attitude is authentic.

"Cassiel?" Kat prompts.

"Expresso. A double," Cass says. Good grief. *Manners*. Did this guy get up on the wrong side of the bed or what? Until now, Troy had the award for being the grumpiest puss in the morning, but Cass was making him look more and more like a saint.

"The usual for me, George." Kat gestures toward double French doors, and I follow Cass into a large office with a comfortable seating area at one end and a round conference table at the other, both in front of large windows. A somewhat messy glass desk and comfy office chair sit between them. Kat leads us to the conference table and sits in the chair in front of a file. Cass and I take the seats on either side of her.

After George brings our coffee and a fresh fruit tray, Kat sits back and smiles, tenting her hands under her chin.

"Let's get right down to business, shall we? I'm sure you're eager to hear how Tommy's doing." Her laugh lines tell me she's probably about ten years older than I am, but you'd never know it from her flawless skin. Quiet confidence and strength ooze from every pore, and I study her in admiration. This woman might very well become my new role model.

"Tommy's been assessed by our child psychologist, and preliminary results show he has PTSD, post-traumatic stress disorder, and a borderline dissociative disorder. He's been through a lot for a ten-year-old. We recommend an intensive rehabilitation program such as ours, where he can grow and heal. Above all, Tommy needs to know he's not alone, so an atmosphere with other children who have had similar experiences would be ideal." Kat taps the file folder. "I have a copy of the results here that you're welcome to take and examine at your leisure. The doctor will be happy to answer all of your questions."

I can't help but be impressed by the concise way she covers all the bases, except for price, all the while her large brown eyes don't seem to miss a trick.

"How is the boy responding so far?" Cass asks. He pulls the folder over and starts to flip through the contents.

"Thankfully, his physical injuries weren't as bad as his abuse would indicate. But, like most do when they first arrive, he tends to keep to himself. He's afraid to trust but seems to have formed an attachment with you," Kat says to Cass, then turns to me. "One thing he has been quite adamant about is expecting a visit from his angel. I assume that's you." She turns her concerned gaze on me. "You've both made quite the impression on the boy."

I nod but keep silent. This meeting gives me a great opportunity to watch Cass and try to figure out what makes him tick. He's proven even harder to get to know than Troy. These three indeed fit the fairy tale rule of three. Cass was the hardest to read, and Tristan the easiest when he isn't blocking me. Troy fit squarely in the middle. Kind of like my own three bears—with all kinds of growl and prickle protecting a sensitive old soul.

Something softer replaces Cass's usual stern demeanor, and I'm finding it very sexy. And trying not to admit that. Because the man has made it more than clear that he has no interest in me and holds me responsible for ruining his relationship with his brother. Usually, when I'm rejected, especially by a man I find attractive, I tuck my tail and race for my safe place. But this time, it's as if there's a tiny seed planted in the chamber of my heart reserved for Cass. A seed that's fighting to sprout. Because of something Nye said about men, or maybe it's just all this superpower stuff. Still, instead of feeling vulnerable and full of shame, his rejection is a challenge… a challenge I might want to win because he's looking all kinds of sexy as he goes into protector mode.

But there is time for all that later. Right now, the universe has brought me here for a reason, and I need to figure out just what that is. So I tune back into the conversation.

"…We recommend our boarding school program for Tommy. Our investigation shows it was Tommy's parents who sold him, so he can't safely return to their residence," Kat says. "Boarding school fees are thirty thousand dollars per semester, and—"

"Cost is not an issue." Cass slides a black Amex across the table. How on frigging earth does an angel get a credit card? "We'll cover the costs for whatever he needs. Now, when can we see him?"

CASSIEL

As soon as Aleah and I enter the private visitors' room, Tommy runs over and wraps his arms around my legs. Despite the treatment center's seventy-two-hour no visitor rule, Kat had let me see the boy on Saturday morning, less than twenty-four hours after we'd found him. Tommy had been terrified and refused to let any of the staff near him without talking to his "angel." He'd finally agreed to talk to me because I was his angel's "warrior."

There'd been some concern about whether a visit from a man might trigger a panic attack, but I'd talked them into giving it a try. Gods know that I'd spent enough time with Atroyel's beloved to know I didn't want to suffer her wrath if I left Tommy on his own. But truth be told, and although it was a millennium ago, I could still remember what it was like to be ripped away from all that I loved and delivered into the hands of strange caregivers. At least I'd had my brothers when our parents died. Right now, we're all Tommy has. His arms wrap around my legs with surprising strength. I bend and lift him into my arms.

"Hey, buddy." I squeeze his small frame. "You doing okay?"

Tommy points to Kat, standing quietly by the door. "I let the nurse give me a bath like I promised."

"I can see that. Good work." I give the scrap of a boy my warmest smile. Removing the layers of dirt that had covered him revealed a stunning biracial child with wide-set blue eyes, a perfectly round face and a head of soft brown curls. Tommy's far smaller than his chronological age would suggest, and I grimace as I feel his ribs through his T-shirt material.

"I'll take this as my cue to leave. If you need anything, pick up the house phone and dial zero, and George will get whatever you need." Kat points to a phone on a small end table and quietly leaves the room. I settle into the love seat beside two floor-to-ceiling windows that look out onto a large field of grazing horses. Aleah takes the seat opposite us.

"You came back, and you brought my angel," Tommy whispers the words in my ear.

"Yes, I did." I look up to see Aleah watching us with that look of empathy that makes my heart constrict. She leans forward and reaches out a hand to Tommy. "Hello there, Tommy. It's terrific to see you again."

Tommy hesitates for a beat then grabs a couple of her fingers. For some reason, maybe because I'm touching Tommy, I can feel the low pulse of healing power worming its way through Tommy as the two remain glued together. Finally, after several long seconds, Aleah squeezes Tommy's fingers.

"You and I have a lot in common," Aleah tells Tommy.

He slowly nods yes.

"Would you like to sit on my lap while I tell you a story? Or you can sit beside me and hold my hand if you prefer."

Aleah scootches back in her love seat and rests an arm along the back, showing Tommy that either choice is okay.

Tommy looks up at me. *Is she a safe adult?*

I give a quick nod that earns me Aleah's look of appreciation, giving my heart another jolt for good measure. If I'm reading her right, she wants to use her new powers to assess Tommy's wounds, so the more skin contact, the stronger the connection.

"Do I still get to be an angel warrior?" Tommy whispers.

"You sure do," Aleah says. "That's a given. You showed us just how brave you are by trusting us and coming here."

I have no idea what the fuck this warrior stuff is about, but Tommy relaxes a bit and moves from my lap to hers. Once he snuggles in, she wraps him in her arms.

"When I was a little girl about your age, I ended up in a foster home where an evil man made me do horrible things that made me very scared and sad. When I told my teacher about it and tried to get help, I got a beating, so I learned to keep my mouth shut," Aleah says. "Do you understand how frightened I was?"

Tommy looks up at her with those solemn eyes and nods.

"So, I kept everything inside and hoped it would all stop, but it didn't. It got worse," Aleah says. "So, I did everything I could to forget, but there was a big hole inside me filled with fear and shame, and the more I tried to forget, the bigger it grew."

"I want to forget all that sticky and disgusting stuff they did to me." Tommy's voice surprises me with its ferocity. The child hasn't spoken above a whisper until now.

Aleah nods, her gaze glued on Tommy's, totally immersed in his world. A tiny voice tries to whisper in the back of my head, but I shut it down. This compassionate side is probably just another of her ruses to trick me into believing she's something that she's not.

"When I look deep into your heart, I see a very brave boy who faced his fears. Do you want to know why a warrior can't forget?" Aleah asks.

Tommy nods.

"An angel warrior needs to be empathetic, and that means he has to appreciate how other people suffer by using his own experiences. I learned that I could ask a trusted adult for help managing the fear and painful memories so I could learn from what happened to me," Aleah says.

"I want to be an angel warrior like Cassiel." Tommy points at me.

Aleah smiles down at him before looking at me with a silent plea. *Are you still willing to help?*

I give a nod of assent as if she's asked aloud. She gives a nod back before directing her gaze back to Tommy.

"Tell you what," she says. "I'll help take away the pain, and you can try what Cassiel and Kat suggest will help you be an angel warrior. How does that sound?"

"What do I have to do?" Tommy sounds skeptical but curious. I give the little guy credit for having the nerve to ask after what he's been through.

"Good for you for asking." Aleah showers him with her approval. "Always ask if you need more information. Here's what we're going to do. I'm new at this angel warrior stuff myself, so you'll need to bear with me, okay?"

Tommy relaxes even more in her arms, now that she's permitted him to make mistakes, and nods.

"Good," Aleah says. "Angels have special powers, and some of them are sharing their magic with me. I want to use it with you. Here's my idea. We'll both hold out our hand." She lifts a hand, and Tommy mirrors her movement. "Now, you think of one of the sticky, disgusting things you want don't want to fear. I'll use my magic to catch it and lock it away. How does that sound?"

I sit forward, curious myself. Putting herself in harm's way by consuming dark ether is either the bravest or stupidest thing I've seen done in eons.

Tommy stares down at his palm for several beats before lowering his chin, tears brimming his eyes. Aleah squeezes him. "I think I almost had it, Tommy. Do you mind trying it again to see if I can catch it this time?"

"Okay." Tommy resettles himself on her lap, and they both stare at his hand again.

This time, strands of dark ether swirl up forming a terrible image. Silent tears run down his face, but he keeps his hand steady. Without taking her eyes from the holograph, Aleah moves her palm close to his. "Now, give it to me."

Tommy hands her the ether, and she clasps the image and, in a flash of light, absorbs it. All three of us sit in stunned silence for several beats, then Aleah and Tommy's faces light with huge smiles. "We did it, bud." She gives him a high five. A shadow briefly flashes in her eyes, but it's gone before I can identify it. Her heartbeat remains steady despite the hit of dark ether. My telepathic perception tells me that Tommy is feeling less fear.

"Let's do it again." Tommy swipes at his tears and holds up his palm.

This time, the image forms almost instantly, and Aleah absorbs it with equal speed. "You're getting good at this, Tommy." They continue with the produce-and-destroy game with such speed that I don't notice the effect it's having on Aleah until she raises her hand, breathless.

"That's a great start for today." Both her heart rate and breathing labor under the strain of battling the dark ether. I stand and take the boy in one arm and reach for her with the other. My gift of empathic healing allows me to heal emotional pain, but I can't touch dark magic. She latches onto my arm with a death grip that's surprisingly strong for someone her size. "Take me home. Now!" Then, she drops to the floor like a stone.

TRISTAN

Alarms clang through our triplet link. Our collective hearts leap into our throats as we rush toward the safe room. I can't be sure where Cass will open the portal, but every fiber tells me something happened, and Aleah will need the safe room. Troy and Raphael, both grim-faced, join me in the hall at the foot of the large circular stairs, and we head out for the magic-protected room.

We've no sooner arrived than Cass steps through a portal, a limp Aleah in his arms. Troy and I stand frozen for several beats, locked in shock and fear. Raphael steps forward and motions toward the bed. "Rest her there."

Cass places Aleah on the bed with uncharacteristic gentleness. Troy and I rush forward as we bark out questions: "What happened? Is she breathing?" Raphael beats us to the punch and stops us in our tracks with a raised hand. Silently, he places a hand on Aleah's forehead for several seconds. When her eyes open, he removes the hand, straightens and stands back. Aleah's alert gaze follows him before sweeping the room.

"Why's everybody looking so morbid?" Nye's voice rings

out loud and clear from near the foot of the bed. "You all look as if someone died. The Chosen is demon drunk, that's all. She has more than enough power to keep the dark magic from doing permanent harm."

Raphael nods. "Until she gains control of her power, she will need assistance ridding herself of the dark magic."

A snort comes from Nye's invisible perch. "What the man's trying to say to you three is that the Chosen needs a good shagging."

Troy and I finish our dash to her side, kneel beside her and touch exposed flesh. There's no barrier to our connection for a change, and Aleah's thoughts and feelings flood through the link. Although I'm not picking up signs of distress, I do a quick assessment of her physical condition. *She's drunk.*

She grins at me and hiccups a nanosecond after the thought forms. "Sure am. I'm drunk and stoned out of my gourd."

"Told you." Nye's voice rings out. "She's demon drunk. It's rare, but we've treated a couple of cases in our time. The dark magic isn't strong enough to poison her like the incubus bite, but it acts as an intoxicant and aphrodisiac until it's dispelled." The sound of clapping hands follows that pronouncement. Troy frowns toward the foot of the bed.

"I don't see the humor in all this, Nye," Troy says. "What are we missing?"

"The magic has powerful truth and confession inducement properties," Raphael says.

"Meaning what?" Cass finds his voice and steps forward.

"Meaning Aleah's under a truth spell that will force her to spill her guts," Nye says. The blank look on Cass's face shows he still can't hear or see the high priestess.

"Ali's under a truth serum," I say.

"I always tell the truth." Aleah wags a finger under Troy's

nose. "Well, almost always. Good thing you're cute." She peels off into a fit of musical laughter.

Troy gets to his feet and dusts his knees off. "She's drunk, all right." He looks at Raphael. "You're sure she's in no danger?"

"Based on our limited experience, I would say not," Raphael says. "However, Domina's powers seem to have magical qualities unique to the Chosen, so there is little supporting our suppositions.

I probably should pay attention to their conversation, but I'm being sucked into the vortex of Ali's heated gaze. As soon as Troy stood, I'd scooted closer to her head to take another quick read on her physical state. She reaches over and rests her hand on my cheek. "I missed you," Ali says in a stage whisper. She then circles her free hand in the air. "Oh, I know I hurt your feelings, and you don't want me anymore, but I sure hope you'll be my friend." Another hiccup. "You're easy to talk to. I miss that the most."

I'm so busy shoring up my heart I almost miss the last few words. Wait, what?

"What did you say?" I hold my breath as I wait for the answer, praying she won't crush my heart yet again.

She grins at me. "I said you're easy to talk to. I'm drunk and stoned, not senile. You're more like Troy than you think."

Just like that, my traitorous heart wants to vault over the wall keeping me from Ali's love.

"Oh, my love—"

"Tristan!" Cass's sharp voice interrupts me shattering the bubbles of hope inspired by Ali's words. "Can we have your attention, please?"

I look up and give him my best W-T-F look as I stand.

"We're debating whether Cass should go or stay and want your take." Troy points his chin toward where Raphael stands at the foot of the bed. "Raphael and Nye say the mansion's magic will work best if only her bonded mates remain in the room."

"And since himself, your alpha has chosen to reject his mate, my vote is for him to sashay his tight little ass right out of this room." Nye's disembodied voice is loud and clear, though it's disconcerting to listen to a voice without a body. For a second I think she's talking about me, but the alpha reference puts her comment squarely on Cass's shoulders.

"I vote Cass stay." Ali's voice is also loud and clear as she struggles to sit up. "Oh fuck. Oh, my gods. Whee!"

Troy and I rush over and sit on either side of her. The moment our flesh meets, the room starts spinning. I send a stream of healing magic through our mating bond, stopping the vertigo.

"That's better," Ali says.

"Maybe you should lie down, beauty," Troy says.

"I'm drunk and stoned, not sick. I'm okay." She pats his arm.

"Time to go," Nye says. "You three can work this out."

"I'll activate the containment spell," Raphael says. "When you are ready, say—"

"*Saor an spiorad* to release the locking spell, we know," Troy says as he walks him to the door.

"Thank you, Rafi," Ali shouts from the bed. "He's cute for an old guy." Another stage whisper, but I catch Raphael's smile as the door closes behind him.

Troy, Cass, and I stand staring at each other for a hot minute. What now?

"Hello, boys." Ali waves from the side of the bed. "I could use a drink, and something's wrong with my legs. Could one of you bring me a drink, please?"

I go to the sideboard and start to pour a glass of water.

"Not water, silly. Wine. Ooops." I turn my head in time to see Ali clap her hands over her mouth.

"I'm so sorry. I shouldn't have called you silly. I wonder if it's shaming to call you guys pet names." She makes a writing motion in the air. "Note to self, ask Brené if using pet names is shaming."

I look over at Troy, and Cass's confusion joins mine through our triplet link.

"I assume she's referring to Brené Brown, some shame researcher she started studying," Troy says.

"Yupper, I'm a Brené Brown apostle," Ali says. "I betcha that's why I'm the Chosen. Because I believe that change starts with each of us." She points her index finger in the general direction of each of us. "The Cosmos chose to give us special gifts so we can spread the word with light, love, and empathy." Wine sloshes in the glass as she takes it from me. "Thank you, Tristan." After slowly enunciating each word, she takes a large sip of the wine.

"Oh, that's good." She yanks on my shirt, and I bend at the waist until my head is inches from hers. "Can you please tell Troy I need to speak with him?" A third stage whisper has her lips puckered and eyes wide.

Troy sits on the other side of her. She does the come-hither thing with her finger, and he lowers his head to hers. I steady her hand as the wine tips precariously, but she doesn't seem to notice.

"I know you don't like surprises, so this is your foreplay warning." She's so theatrical it's hard not to laugh. "We need to get rid of your brothers so we can do the deed."

Troy's unique brand of humor trickles through our link. "Are you sure about that, babe? I thought you wanted to try another threesome."

She takes another sip of the wine while she studies him. "I do, but your brothers *rejected* me, so there go my wet dreams about more threesomes." A sad little smile hits her full lips. "Do you know why they don't like me?"

I open my mouth to protest, but Troy beats me to the punch as he deftly removes the wine glass and holds it out for Cass to take. "Their loss, beauty. I don't want to talk about my brothers right now."

A flush of sensual heat floods through our mating bond as Ali's smile transforms her face. "Oh, and just what do you want to talk about?" she asks playfully.

You're easy to talk to. I miss that the most. Ali's words are an anthem of joy set on repeat, and the feeling flooding through our bond seals my fate. I've got to have her again.

ALEAH

I'm demon drunk. I decide Nye's term for my condition fits because only something evil could make me feel this good and bad at the same time. Something decidedly unpleasant is pulsing through my system, and it's making me so horny that it's hard to focus on anything else. The part of my brain that filters my verbal outbursts is on hiatus. There's a tug of war happening with my libido on one side, and the urge to vomit out every last thought in my head on the other, and it nauseates me. Literally.

I focus on Troy's hot gaze as a distraction from the cyclone of shit going on in my body. If I was in my right mind, I wouldn't have asked him what he wants to talk about because he usually wants to talk about one of two things, my sexual fantasies or my sexual desires. But the vibe coming through my link isn't the one of intense passion indicating Troy is in the right mood.

"Maybe he just needs a little nudge." I'm not sure if the echoey voice sounding in my head belongs to Nye or the house, but either way, it's wrong.

"So, I'm not going to get lucky, and you don't want to talk

about your brothers and why they rejected me. What then?" I don't even try to keep the tone of sarcastic ire from my voice. Hell, I'd throw in an eye roll or two if I wasn't so damned demon drunk. *Wait, are demons evil?*

"Beauty, you got lucky the day we met." Troy's eyes twinkle with that devilish glee of his. "But if you're asking if I'm going to fuck you, the answer is when the time is right. And no, all demons aren't evil, but most are. Some are simply passive."

I shoot every bit of mock hatred I have at him knowing our link tells him it's all in jest. "Bastard." Trust Troy to carry his "right-time attitude" into the afterlife. "And stop reading my mind."

Troy winks. "But I'm cute, and I'm not reading your mind. You asked if demons are evil using your outdoor voice."

"Good thing you're cute" is a put-down disguised as a compliment an acquaintance repeatedly used with her boy-toy husband and one we've used as a joke ever since. I play slap his arm or attempt to, but air replaces his arm and my strike misses. I lose my balance and start to fall backward. *Oh fuck, I'm going to spill my wine.* No sooner has that thought hit that I realize my wine is nowhere to be found. Troy wraps his beautifully molded arm around my shoulder and pulls me back up to a sitting position.

"To answer your question, I want you to talk to my brothers and clear the air. You don't cope at all well with emotional conflict, and you won't be able to focus on figuring out this Chosen stuff until you work this out. At the very least, you should make an attempt with Tristan. Whatever's going on between you two can't continue." Troy's in full won't-budge mode, so there's no point arguing with him. And he's right. He knows better than anyone the way I respond when I'm having some kind of internal conflict. The longer I try to avoid it, the sicker I'll get.

But what the fuck can I say to these two? I lean my head on Troy's shoulder and let out a heavy sigh, knowing there's no point in putting off arguing. Troy has a single-minded devotion to the cause once he decides an emotional issue needs examining.

I crane my neck to sneak a peek at Tristan and damn near break my neck trying.

"I have an idea." Tristan's smoky tenor distracts me with the usual Pavlovian squirt of moisture between my legs because there's no other explanation for me missing how I've changed position. Yet, here I am, magically propped against pillows with Tristan sitting cross-legged on the bed beside me. Looking at me and sucking me into the vortex of those blue eyes. Suddenly, it's as if the room shrinks, and we are the only two remaining sentient beings in the universe.

I stare back, thoughts flipping through my mind so fast they trip each other up. Every single cell in my body screams that this is one of those chances for me to grab the brass ring. The way I'd done with Troy all those years ago, despite what logic and warnings to the contrary. I'm suddenly sure that, like then, if I walk away from this moment, I'll regret it the rest of my life. Taking the leap with Troy has been the best thing I'd ever done, so why wouldn't it be the same with Tristan? But how do I tell him my doubts and dreams without shaming him? How do I make him see how hurt I am by his rejection despite my bravado?

"Tell him you love him." The house and Nye nudge me. But that's the one area where I won't stick my neck out, not ever. I'd stubbornly held on until Troy told me he loved me despite knowing deep down that I could have saved him a great deal of emotional angst and a couple of years. Rejection triggers my shame on the deepest level, and perhaps that's my deepest

secret. The whole world thinks I'm strong and can handle anything and there's a significant degree of truth to that, but that strength leaves also leave me vulnerable. Something only Troy knows about me.

So, I say the first stupid thing that pops into my head. "Why did you stop calling me *mon chou?*" Unbidden tears spring to my eyes, but I can't analyze the reason for them right now. Not at this life-changing moment. Every fucking aching thing in my body—my brand, heart and soul—tells me I'm on the verge of something enormous, something vital. Our eyes stay locked for several eternities.

"It's complicated, and I don't want to go into it right now. What do you want to talk to me about?" His voice is so low I almost miss it. Two frown lines matching mine crease his forehead. Some basic need within him reaches out to me, showing me what he's really asking. *Why do you need me?*

There are so many things; where do I start? Because more than anything, I want that feeling I had when we were on the Santiagos' island. There, I'd been the only person in his universe. When his smile and musical laugh sent warm sensual pixie dust down to my toes, so expressive and full of passion. He'd leaned in whenever I made a point, receptive but without the edge of skepticism that Troy brought to most conversations.

"Stop being such a ninny and just start talking, for fuck's sake." Nye's voice rings loudly in my head. "Can't you see the wee lad is on the verge of breaking?"

My aching head stops me from another eye roll. Nye and I would have a chat later about what makes Tristan so special to her. I can't avoid him any longer. The heat from his blue eyes makes my lady bits do another cha-cha, but Tristan has a lot more patience than Troy does. He sits there looking at me, a tiny smile I can't interpret tugging at the corner of his lips. What do I want to talk to him about?

"Nothing and everything," I finally choke out.

His smile widens. "Okay, let's start with one thing."

Oh gods, how I want to reach out and trace the smile lines framing his lips. I clutch my hands tightly in my lap to keep from touching him.

"Would you two stop fucking around and get on with it?" Troy's voice bursts through our bubble, startling both of us, judging by the expression on Tristan's face. Cass is radio silent.

"Fine, fine. Fuck off," I say grumpily. I take a deep breath. Okay, here goes. But before I can act, Tristan grabs both cheeks, and electricity flows through our link. Despite a few desperate attempts, I can't hide the thoughts and feelings I've hidden bubbling like hot lava deep in the well of not-enough. Hurt at his lack of trust joins rejection as our gazes remain locked. The same strong emotions flow back at me, although their source catches me by surprise. A slideshow I don't recall starts showing a younger version of me trotting after Troy in various settings… oblivious to Tristan in the background.

You always chose Troy first. All I'm suitable for is a good lay.

The force of Tristan's feelings brings tears to my eyes, and I reach for him.

TRISTAN

A torrent of unfiltered emotion floods through our link, so strong it's like walking into a typhoon. Ali's fears, hopes, needs, and a trench of deep love and empathy course through me. The assault of emotions is almost more than I can bear as Ali's authentic inner self flows into me, showing a love for me that's as strong as, although different from her love for Troy. With loving force, she blasts through my resistance and invades that place deep within that I've hidden from every living being, even my brothers. The brand on my shoulder burns as if hit with a bolt of her white-blue heat. A distant voice tries to warn me against going any further, but it's too late for that.

"My God, you're beautiful." Desire licks at me like the touch of a match igniting a fuse.

Her brown eyes, luminous in the dim light, shine with anticipation.

Ali pulls my face to hers. Her lips devour mine as she rips at my shirt in a fever of expectation. Even though my need is as urgent and savage as hers, I put my hands on her shoulders to still her.

"Slowly." I caress the side of her face and tuck a tendril of hair behind her ear.

She shivers at my touch. "I want you, Tristan." She clutches the back of my head and pulls it toward hers.

"Shhh." I hold her at arm's length. "Not another word."

Ali whimpers. Every fiber of her being trembles with impatience, and I smile again. This time I know that she'll speak her love through her body, and I can't wait to hear what she has to say.

Using my fingertips, I draw the angles of her face and delicately skim the ovals of her eyes, the rounded tip of her nose, and the lushness of her lips. When I stroke the backs of her delicate ears, she moans. My skin heats at the sound. I inhale deeply to still the fire threatening to consume me. Her dark curls cascade around her face. I take a handful, tip her head, and bring her lips to mine.

I trace and retrace the outline of her mouth with the tip of my tongue, eager to remember every contour of her exquisite mouth. Finally, Ali's tongue joins mine, sending a jolt of lust through my aching hardness. She presses into me, and I grab her wrists.

Her impatience and longing bleed through our link. She slides down the bed, and I pull her arms above her head and hold them with one hand at her wrists before sliding my lips along the length of her neck. A wisp of her perfume makes me stiffen more, but I keep the reins on my control. Using my free hand and magic, I strip off our clothes while I gaze into her sparkling eyes, measuring her response while I toss each piece to the floor.

Ali's small breasts are magnificent, and I pause to admire them. My pulse quickens, and my tattoo throbs unbearably, but I manage to continue the measured pace of my breathing. I let go of her wrists and cup each of the soft globes in my hand. Stifling a sigh, I study the way her tawny skin contrasts with the darker hue of her large, brown nipples. Ali lets out a low moan as my tongue circles each hard bud before sucking them deeply, first one and then the other. She arches her back and wraps her legs around my ass. I lick and gently tug each plump berry until she goes taut with longing.

Straightening, I look into her eyes and am rewarded with tortured anticipation. I take a moment to admire the perfection of her smooth, dark skin against the brilliant-white duvet. Troy is right in his assessment. Our Ali's smooth skin is a work of art or quite possibly one of the wonders of the world.

Her need surrounds me, threatening to consume me. The look in her eyes begs me for release, but despite the urgent pull coming through our brand, I want this moment to last for eternity. Her soft flesh warms as I explore the curve of her abdomen and the insides of her thighs. My fingers come away wet with her desire.

She spreads her legs wide for me, giving me the full view of her manicured pussy. I dance my finger across her clit. A small groan of satisfaction I can't suppress rumbles from the back of my throat. She moans and wraps her legs around me again, tightening the grip of her thighs, pulling me closer. I put a finger over my lips to still her, despite the urgent pull coming from my brand.

"This time, I want to pleasure you."

Her sultry lips are plump with her longing. I bend and brush them with mine before turning my attention to her glistening folds. I sandwich her crimson bud between two fingers, and her legs part, inviting me to devour her. With a growl, I kneel between her legs. Bending, I pull her rigid clit into my mouth, torn by my desire to taste her and the satisfaction of watching her come.

The need to have her pulses through me. I thrust two fingers into the wetness flowing from her before licking her essence from them. *Gods, she tastes good.* Fingering her again, I press on her swollen G-spot, pushing upward while also rubbing the bud between the engorged petals of her nether lips. Ali's eyes close. She arches on the bed, her lashes fanning her cheeks. And I feel the first spasm as my body screams for release.

Focus, dammit, focus!

I take a deep breath and reach for the steel core of my control. Ali pants and writhes. I take my time, determined to take her to the highest peak, the ultimate climax. I stroke, squeeze, and stroke some more until her body goes rigid, dripping with sweat.

"Please," she begs. "Please, Tristan." Her Nephilim grace joins mine, mingling in the air to form a beautifully intricate pattern.

I look up, savoring the sexual power I exert as she twists in her eagerness. I want this woman and her ability to lose herself to her desire. This time there's no doubt that desire is for me, body and soul. I'm finally home after being lost in a world of obscurity. My brand sends a flood of endorphins through my system as if in agreement.

Again, I dip my head and take her pulsing clitoris into my mouth, torturing it to its full extension. I slow my pace; we have all the time in the world. Once again, I press my fingers hard against the roof of her vagina. Ali lies suspended as if life itself is too much. Then, with a raw cry, she clenches. The power of her orgasm jolts through me, and her contractions crush my fingers.

I fight the animal urge to rut between her legs, of letting my hot seed pump into her. I want my body to give her the answer she deserves after the shit I've put her through with my rejection. Withdrawing my fingers from her slippery cunt, I brush them across her lips, reveling in her eagerness to taste what she's so openly given me. She sucks greedily, devouring every bit of her delicious cum from my fingers. My penis almost bursts with the agony of my erection, yet still, I'm patient.

Heavy with arousal, my cock answers Ali's groan. I heft my bursting rod. Slowly, deliberately, I kneel again between her legs. She grabs my ass. My balls contract. Pulling her arms above her head again, I pin her wrists with one hand and use the other to grasp one of her breasts. Then, with a single thrust, I drive into her.

She slowly enfolds me, wrapping herself around me, a lock receiving the key designed for it. Her engorged core is everything I remember and so much more. Heat and hot light stream from our mating brands, bringing a moment I want to preserve for all time.

I hold myself rigid and resist the beginnings of the orgasm deep within. I'm not sure how much longer I can endure, but I'm determined to enjoy every moment in Ali's cunt as if it's my last. So, with purposeful restraint, I plunge inside her, deep and hard, slow and long, never once taking my eyes off her. I love watching her writhe with greed for me.

I stroke, sometimes slowly, sometimes with mad abandon, each time, stopping myself before I reached the point of no return. Finally, Ali goes rigid again, signaling the time to embrace our mutual release. As she howls with her climax, I clench, draw in my breath, and lose myself as I erupt into oblivion.

Throwing my head back, I gasp for air while Ali's warmth enhances my pleasure. I've waited so long to touch her, yet nothing prepared me for the intensity of our reunion. She pulls me down on her. I still, enjoying the crush of her breasts against my chest. We lay, heart to heart, surrounded by a curtain of divine light.

I cling to the moment as if the hope of having joy in my

life depended on it. Rolling onto my back, I draw her into the crook of my arm. When she tucks her head under my chin, I bury my nose in her hair, inhaling deeply. Her scent carries everything I'll ever need to survive. She runs her slender fingers through the dusting of chest hair circling my nipples, sighing.

"Body and soul," she says. "I wish we could stay like this forever."

A feeling of unfinished business washes over me, compelling me to roll us onto our sides. The curtain of light parts, and I look up to see Troy, our missing piece. Giving me a smile of pure brotherly love, he climbs onto the bed and spoons Aleah from behind. The curtain closes around us and becomes a wall of divine light and love… with Cass on the outside swimming in a vat of fear.

Find out what happens to Aleah and her angels in *Tristan*, the conclusion of the Rogue Angels series!

Join Lilith's Smutty Readers Email List and get a free copy of *Mick's Mission*, a paranormal reverse harem romance!

lilithdarville.com/newsletter

Chapter One
Cassiel

"Fuck!" Shame and fear consume me as I bounce off the curtain of light surrounding my brothers and Aleah as a divine mating bond binds the three of them. I arrive a split second too late to stop Aleah from stealing my brothers from me. Now, it's up to me to save them. And myself. I refuse to take too close a look at precisely what I'm saving them from. If I do that, I might have to admit a truth or two I refuse to acknowledge.

Rage swamps over me as I watch the three of them linked, locked and awash in divine love. Love and desire bleed through our triplet link in nauseating quantities. This couldn't have happened; shouldn't have happened. Nothing was supposed to be strong enough to shatter the triplet bond between the royal princes of the Blue Vale.

Maybe Lord Syrael was right about her.

Where the fuck did that come from? I give my head a

shake. Ever since Aleah rescued that child slave Tommy, I've been getting flashes better left forgotten.

Fueled by anger that's building to an inferno, I stalk from the room. One of us has to be fucking responsible here, and as usual, that job falls on my shoulders. Aleah's detailed agenda that she was so fucking kind to share with us advises she's touring some private membership club for her gods-damned article. It falls to me to do the fucking prework my brothers should have done. The fucking assholes should know better than let their libidos take priority over the mission to protect Aleah from Lord Syrael at all costs.

"Turn her over to me. You'll get your brothers back, and I'll set you free."

I could swear I hear a deep voice whispering those words in my head, but the thought is gone before I can grasp it. Yet it's happening more and more, these dark threads filtering through my thoughts. Then there's the constant hum of heat from our triplet link that's taken hold of my junk. It's jerking me one way and the dark threads another. It's enough to make an angel batshit crazy and lets me know I *need* to get laid. I can kill the proverbial two birds with one visit to Pandemonium—scout the location and scene with a hot sub.

I stop by my assigned bedroom to take off my jacket and shed my tie in a nod to a more casual look. Wearing one of my signature custom suits to scene at a sex club in the middle of the night is more than a bit of overkill. I'll be there to survey, not announce my presence, and the high-noon gunslinger look of the 1920's style clothing I favor makes a statement. So, I tone it down. Many there will be wearing fetish gear, but that's not my style.

Raphael waits near the door as I step into the main hall, my long outer coat slung carefully over his extended arm.

"Thank you." I stride forward, and he holds the coat open

for me to shrug on. Seeing the caretaker waiting as if he reads my mind startles me, but I'm a master at hiding my reactions from everyone, friend or foe.

Raphael raises his palm, and a small vial appears. The nectar inside the vial cloaks our divine grace and magic.

I shake my head and wave a hand, dismissing the idea. "Thanks, but I won't be needing that." My tone makes it clear this is not up for discussion. I have more than enough power to suppress my magic, making it undetectable. If I choose to.

Raphael bows his head slightly and the vial disappears. "As you wish."

"I'll be at the Pandemonium club getting us registered. I'll be back in a couple of hours." I open a portal before he can argue with me and step through into the shadows outside of the private sex club. After explaining my visit to reception, a "serving wench" named Darcy escorts me around the premises. She points out various rooms and explains the pandemic protocols they practice, eventually stopping in the primary dungeon. The social area is full of people in various stages of undress and fetish gear chatting and watching the scenes in the adjoining play area. My attention is immediately drawn to the bondage equipment on a far wall as a large man sidles up beside me.

"Most of the furniture is unique and custom-built for The Woodshed." The man is shorter than me, but his commanding presence quickly identifies him as a Dom. "My name is Master Zazz. Welcome to our dungeon. The front desk tells me Cyrus Stone referred you to us." The inflection in his tone doesn't rise, but there's no doubt the man expects an answer. He gives Darcy a nod, and she strides off toward the reception area.

"Indirectly, yes." I match my tone to his. "I'm here to scout the location on behalf of Mosaic Magazine and their contributor, Aleah Hunter. She's writing a feature series on Cyrus Stone and his Pleasure Palace." I stop short of opining on how a man with so little imagination can run a sex empire.

Zazz, massive arms crossed over his barrel chest, stares and waits. I stifle my impatience. Getting on this guy's wrong side will no doubt piss Aleah right off. The thought of her petite body facing off with me once again without fear makes my cock go rock hard. I push the thought away needing to focus on the play before me.

"Are those modified St. Andrew's Crosses?" I point to the bondage furniture lining the wall. Since flogging and whipping are my favorite forms of impact play, I'm particularly interested in bondage furniture. And having Aleah's naked body splayed out on it. Again, my cock goes harder still, and I pull my long coat closed. Unlike the exhibitionists in the crowd, I prefer to choose how I display myself in public.

Zazz's lips quirk into a smile as if letting me know I'm not fooling him for a second. He's seen it all before and then some, I have no doubt. He nods. "The design is a hybrid between a St. Andrew's Cross and another piece we developed called the Stickman. They're comfortable for your bottom and very stable."

I give a nod to acknowledge his subtle identification of a fellow Dom. "I look forward to giving it a try."

The tour continues, and Zazz points out various points of evident pride. I listen impatiently as he holds forth about the shibari rigs and rope play, but that's Tristan's kink, not mine. However, the custom spanking benches do capture my attention. Another image of Aleah, this time kneeling on the red leather, legs spread wide on the spanking bench, keeps my cock standing at attention.

After noting the bootblack stand for later use, Zazz spends a few moments pointing out the features of an updated suspension cage. Again, not my usual kink as I have no patience for protracted punishment play.

Darcy comes up behind Zazz and stands demurely, head down in submission until he gestures for her to speak. She slides closer and whispers in his ear.

"Ah, good," Zazz says. "Sensei Master Stone happens to be on the premises, and he's eager to meet one of the Mosaic Magazine's entourage."

My heart rate accelerates at the mention of his name. I put it down to Zazz's unusual use of the title *sensei master*. The title lets me know that Cyrus Stone considers himself a BDSM king.

Zazz leads the way down a long hall, opens the door to a private playroom and steps back, gesturing for me to go inside. Eager to meet the kingpin and set the ground rules, I walk forward, barely registering the door closing behind me.

A large man sits on an oversized padded chair upon a raised platform, like a throne on a dais. Muscular legs are spread wide, and a hairy forearm sits on each throne's arm, a bullwhip curled in one hand. As our eyes meet, his glow with an ethereal black light. Images of the time when he had guardianship over me and my brothers comes flooding back. It's as if he rips away the bandage hiding the festering boil of dark magic that he planted in my soul to make me submit to being a plaything for him and his friends. Fear and loathing swarm through me as his dark power pours over me, taking control of my muscles and mind.

"Kneel, Cassiel. Bow to your master." His deep voice brings back another torrent of images from the torture I endured as a child. Torture I suffered at the hands of him and his patrons to save my brothers from a similar fate. I lock my knees, refusing to bow, ignoring the fear choking off my air supply. I'm no longer that boy.

I hear the snap a split second before the pain hits the

tender spot at the back of my knees. I drop to the floor, bowing to Cyrus Stone.

End of Sample
To continue reading, be sure to pick up *Tristan* at your favorite retailer.

ALSO BY LILITH DARVILLE

Wicked Angels Series

Dark Urban Fantasy Romance

Interconnected Standalones

Follow a team of fallen angels as they fight against human trafficking and navigate the blurred lines between good and evil. Set in Pandemonium, a notorious club where they blend in with humans, this heart-pounding series will leave you breathless. Don't miss out on this intense and spicy journey of redemption and second chances.

.

Rogue Angels Series

Dark Urban Fantasy Romance

Completed Series

Rogue Angels is a twist retelling of the Snow White fairytale. Enjoy an adventure with fated mates, midlife crisis, and evil demons. This story includes themes of love, sacrifice, and self-discovery.

.

Sexy Sins Afterlife Retreat Series

Paranormal Reverse Harem Romance

Completed Series

Warning: This series has one strong woman and four dangerously sexy immortal men. She's been their fated mate in every life they've lived and they refuse to live one without her. Read this series if you like why choose romance with a paranormal twist and hunky guys times four!

.

Masquerade Club Series

Dark Contemporary Romance

Completed Series

A contemporary saga with a side dish of spice and a second chance romance for two people you'll never forget. The Masquerade Club is exclusive and available only for the ultra-rich where all your dreams and fantasies come true. Join the party and fall in love with Connor and Katherine in this angst-ridden suspense-filled series.

.

ABOUT THE AUTHOR

Lilith Darville is a *USA Today* bestselling author of dangerously delicious romance, including sizzling paranormal reverse harem. With over forty years of storytelling experience, her stories are guaranteed to make readers flush and blush.

lilithdarville.com